PRAISE FOR *PANICS*

"These surreal, claustrophobic stories bear similarities to the works of Samuel Beckett and Leonora Carrington, but Molinard writes in a voice that is entirely her own. . . . Through Ramadan's spare and exacting translation, Molinard presents a terrifying portrait of violence and mental illness."
—*NEW YORK TIMES*

"The thirteen stories in *Panics*—rendered into beautiful, plain-spoken English by translator Emma Ramadan, and by turns surreal, mesmerizing, and darkly unhinged—bear the mark of their writer's painstaking process."
—*ASTRA MAGAZINE*

"Dispensing with the ordinary rules of time, space, and motivation that govern our everyday, [Molinard] calls into question just what it means to be human."
—*BOMB*

"Startling and surreal. . . . Ramadan's translation is a great gift to readers."
—*PUBLISHERS WEEKLY* (starred review)

"Like the disembodied hands and faceless lovers in these stories, there is as much presented as there is withheld in *Panics*, Barbara Molinard's singular collection. Marguerite Duras tells us that Molinard destroyed most of her own writing, and I'm fascinated by what's left out, what's left unseen, in this essential text."
—STEPHANIE LACAVA, author of
I Fear My Pain Interests You

"To read Barbara Molinard's surreal, tormented, tender, and brutal stories is to dive into the wreck and then witness a singular talent at work. Lucid, horror-drenched, droll, absurd, *Panics* is perfect reading for the nightmare that is the present. A shriek from the archives, a gift to us all."

—SARAH THANKAM MATHEWS, author of
All This Could Be Different

"With its unique, haunting imagery and Kafkaesque momentum, *Panics* reads like a series of lucid dreams. A gleaming, razor-sharp book that has lost none of its edge in Emma Ramadan's masterful English translation."

—OLIVIA BAES, cotranslator of *Me & Other Writing*

"Notorious for having destroyed most of her writing, Barbara Molinard has given us a sacred gift in *Panics*. These stories are rendered with a mastery that directly conveys the preciousness of life. At the end, I found myself in a bit of panic, so to speak—how to go on having seen something so gorgeous?"

—MORGAN TALTY, author of *Night of the Living Rez*

BARBARA MOLINARD

Panics

STORIES

PRECEDED BY A PREFACE
BY MARGUERITE DURAS
AND FOLLOWED BY
A STORY IMPROVISED
BY BARBARA MOLINARD
AND TRANSCRIBED
BY MARGUERITE DURAS

*Translated from the French
by Emma Ramadan*

THE FEMINIST PRESS
AT THE CITY UNIVERSITY OF NEW YORK
NEW YORK CITY

Published in 2022 by the Feminist Press
at the City University of New York
The Graduate Center
365 Fifth Avenue, Suite 5406
New York, NY 10016
feministpress.org

First Feminist Press edition 2022

This book was made possible thanks to a grant from the New York State Council on
the Arts with the support of the Governor and the New York State Legislature.

ART WORKS.
arts.gov

This book is supported in part by an award from the National Endowment for the Arts.

Second printing February 2023

Cover design by Sukruti Anah Staneley
Cover art by Rozenn Le Gall
Interior artwork by Barbara Molinard
Text design by Drew Stevens

Library of Congress Cataloging-in-Publication Data is available for this title.

ISBN 978-1-55861-295-2

PRINTED IN THE USA BY McNAUGHTON & GUNN, A WOMEN-OWNED BUSINESS.

CONTENTS

PREFACE

Barbara Molinard lives in a large house in the countryside. She's there alone twelve hours a day. She's been writing for eight years.

What we've collected in this book represents a very small portion—maybe a hundredth—of what Barbara has written over these eight years. The rest was destroyed.

Barbara writes. And she tears to shreds. She continues, she writes. And the other person, whom she refers to (for the past few months now) as her "enemy," tears up what she's written.

EVERYTHING BARBARA MOLINARD HAS WRITTEN HAS BEEN TORN TO SHREDS.

The texts that follow were also torn to shreds. They were put back together, torn up again, put back together again. How many times? Even she doesn't know. As many times as NECESSARY, which is to say until she was in agony, until meaning was plunged back into the absolute night of its source, the mother of suffering.

Barbara tears to shreds just as carefully as she writes, according to a method. Each page is ripped into four pieces. Those pieces piled up form a whole. That whole, those piles—intermediaries—between the ashes and the page, remain on her table, before her eyes, for a certain amount of time. Then into the fire, I believe.

Once, Barbara wrote the entire day for five weeks straight—on vacation, at a hotel—then destroyed everything as usual and didn't remember a thing. Those absolute losses are relatively numerous.

Before this collection came together, her suffering reached its peak when the need to destroy swooped down on Barbara and she struggled against herself, with all her might—for then, having OBEYED, she could rest. It's thanks to this rest that she was able to start again and then to hope, to escape from the enemy, from the murderer who, every day, inspected her desk and assassinated everything.

That rest, that hope, in fact merely gave her a new opportunity to destroy. This lasted eight years.

For eight years, her husband and I have countered Barbara's enemy with the vulgarity of life. We are not unaware of the violence we did by begging her—regularly— to "SEPARATE" herself from her texts, to put them out of reach of her enemy, for example, at a publishing house. She, even as her body rebelled, called for something new. The infernal cycle of her suffering had to change. Suffering endures and will endure. But it will strike elsewhere, and it's this novelty that Barbara used to her advantage.

She agreed. She handed over the texts.

I knew, because I had read them—previously—that there were still more texts she hadn't handed over. I insisted. She refused. This went on for several months. It was just before publication that suddenly she brought them, the following four texts: "Come," "The Father's Apartment," "The Bed," "The Sponge." Those four texts Barbara WITHHELD are not fundamentally different than the texts Barbara RELIN-QUISHED. But the enemy had to have its lifeblood and no doubt they were kept to be offered up as sacrifice.

As for the text titled "The Vault," Barbara had renounced writing it—after several attempts—and so we tried to reconstruct the plot together. We did so in a single session, without any issues. This ACCOUNT had to be written down, if only to hoist it beyond the inexpressible.

Barbara dreams of a house other than the one she has. The house exists, she says; she can describe it. It's an enclosed tower that gets no light except during "days of suffering." In that tower she would live alone and no one would come looking for her. She feels her actual house is too open, too exposed to others.

In that tower she would write.

What readers will find here is neither invented nor dreamed. It's a record of lived experience. Writing is a part of that. Writing is lived. It is a step in the walk of suffering. Without it, the constant suffering would not have been bearable. Of that I am sure.

Sometimes Barbara finds herself terrified, out of nowhere, in the street, by a face, a face that no one else seems to notice. The resulting affliction can last days. The shock can be so unbearable that she flees. She flees with the face she saw, she brings it back home with her. There, she stares at it. She stares at it until she has confirmed the intolerable nature of all life.

Other times Barbara sees a negated face. And then what she brings home with her is the desperation to replace it with a lively face. In the remarkable coherence of the general incoherence, suffering is the cement. Between the terrifying face and the nothing face, the cement is Barbara's suffering.

The human race is flawed. The cities are flawed. The modes of transportation are all wrong: either you miss them or they don't bring you where you want to go. A few confident people roam through this universe, never cured of their loving, their serving, their waiting.

—MARGUERITE DURAS
1969

THE PLANE FROM SANTA ROSA

Excuse me, sir, what time does the plane from Santa Rosa arrive? After consulting the schedule, the employee answered that the plane from Santa Rosa would land at 7:50 p.m. The woman also wanted to know what time the plane would take off from Santa Rosa, how many stops it would make, and the length of each one. The employee looked into it, made several phone calls, and once this information had been communicated, the woman then wanted to know how many passengers would be on the plane, if the weather forecast was good, and finally, if there was any reason to fear an accident. Growing impatient, the employee pointed out to her that there were other people waiting their turn, and that in any event, he wasn't qualified to answer such questions. Slightly flustered, the woman excused herself with a smile, thanked him, and left.

Outside, she hesitated for a moment about which way to go. She decided to turn right, take the first street on the left, continue straight, and turn left again. She was surprised to find herself in front of her building. She went up to the third floor, took her key from her bag, turned it in the lock of the door on the left side of the landing, and entered her room: a bed on the right, next to the bed a small chair serving as a nightstand, a closet in the back, a few dresses on hangers, a coat, a sink, to the left a hot plate on a small table, a cabinet. Lazily she walked to the bed, sat down, let her legs hang, leaned against the wall, and remained perfectly still. This dead time when she returned home had become a part of her routine, waiting . . . waiting. Everything became muddled, impalpable, distant. It took a lot of willpower not to let herself be overtaken by that torpor. Most often, objects would get her back on task. The alarm clock, which she glanced at in passing, brought her back to reality. She reminded herself abruptly that she had no time to lose. She still had several things to do before the plane arrived; she had to hurry. In front of the mirror, she adjusted the hat she hadn't taken off, brushed off her coat, and left, carefully locking the door behind her.

On the boulevard, she walked rapidly, like someone in a rush. From time to time, she'd stop in front of a store, hastily glance at the window, and immediately carry on again. She lingered in front of a particular storefront and, after a few moments of consideration, resolutely entered the store. She was greeted by an opulent and prickly salesclerk. The woman pointed to the dress in the window and asked to try it on. With hostility, the salesclerk removed the dress and handed it to the woman. After she had tried it on, the woman wanted to see others . . . and still others. But there was always something not quite right. The salesclerk was growing impatient, but still the woman continued, trying on dress after dress and seeming not to notice. Then, once she'd had enough, the salesclerk made a few disagreeable remarks. As if to excuse herself, the woman explained that she had an important dinner that very night . . . friends were arriving on the plane from Santa Rosa, and that was why the dress had to be just right . . . there was no time for alterations. The salesclerk gave an impertinent laugh at these explanations. Mildly disconcerted, the woman nevertheless tried on one or two more dresses before leaving the store empty-handed. The door slammed on her heels.

On the boulevard, she began walking quickly again, seemingly unaware of the rain that was starting to fall. After a brief inner struggle in front of a furrier, she entered the store. The person who greeted her, very familiar with her clientele, diagnosed right away that this woman was not a serious customer, but she couldn't refuse to show her the pieces in the collection that she asked to see. As the furs passed over her shoulders, the woman's back hunched more and more, as if weighed down by a heavy burden. The more furs she tried on, the more her back hunched, imperceptibly. The woman felt an enormous surge of fatigue that pushed her to the brink of vertigo. She wished she could admit defeat, put an end to it all, but she continued to try on the furs, one after another, stubborn. It seemed out of her control to stop what had become a nightmarish scene. It might have lasted until she collapsed from exhaustion if the salesclerk, concerned about the large drops of sweat she saw beading on the woman's face, had not asked her to rest for a moment. As she was walked to the door, the woman feebly tried to explain Santa Rosa . . . the plane . . . her friends . . . the dinner . . .

On the boulevard, she headed toward a bench, there, just opposite, and sat down in a stupor. A beggar, a sort of vagabond, took a seat next to her, so close that their elbows touched. The man carefully opened a greasy old newspaper on his knees and started to rummage through some food scraps; he tore off the last clinging bits of meat from a bone with evident delight. The woman's eyes automatically went from the remnants of food in the newspaper to the man's face. In her mind's great confusion, she felt vaguely envious of him.

Then, her mind blank, she watched the passersby. Two sailors, arm in arm, were zigzagging along the sidewalk; a woman was pushing a stroller, beaming a thousand smiles to a chubby-cheeked baby batting the air with his hands; a wispy blond, hanging on the arm of a large man with slicked-back hair, was laughing with all her teeth bared; children, schoolbags under their arms, were biting into apple turnovers. Men . . . children . . . women . . . children . . . women . . . a hoop . . . a kite—the plane! Suddenly frantic, the woman jumped up from the bench, crossed the road, took the street to the right, to the left, straight, this street, that street. Now she was almost running, so afraid was she of being late. 7:50 p.m.! Would she ever arrive? Three floors, the key in the lock, the room. The cold water, the soap, the toothbrush invigorated her. Standing in front of the mirror, she quickly smoothed her hair, grabbed the shiny coat that she wore for special occasions, tried to find a pair of tights with no runs in them, grabbed her bag, and left.

She ran to the metro, got on, and once she'd found a seat was finally able to breathe. She consulted the map and counted twelve stops until the station where she would catch a bus that would take her to another bus that would, at last, bring her to the airport. The trip seemed endless. She was so afraid of being late, and she was so tired. The fear of missing the plane's arrival filled her with panic. Standing in the metro, legs limp and hands trembling, she clung to the railing so she wouldn't fall.

7:50 p.m.! The engine thrummed and the plane landed. She had arrived.

In the middle of the crowd, she waited for the passengers to walk off the plane. The first, the next, and the last crossed the gangway. Standing on tiptoe, the woman watched them attentively, one by one. All around her, arms raised and hands waved: a silent language to express the impatience to embrace. The woman also raised and waved her hands, thus melding into the joy of all and the happiness of each. After the customs formalities, the passengers were finally free. There were kisses, smiles, tears of joy, and bursts of laughter; friendly words and loving, tender words. There was all of it. All. The woman saw all of it. All.

Now alone, in the middle of the deserted terminal, she thought that it was time to go home. The rain on the other side of the glass must have been responsible for the curtain of haze muddling her view.

The bus, the other bus, and the metro. The street to the left, to the right, straight ahead, and left again. The stairs, the door, the key, the lock, her room.

Seated on the bed, her back against the wall and her legs dangling, she surrendered to the passing time, to the dead time she knew so well and from which she was forever forced to flee in order not to die. She conceded that she had no reason to complain about her day: she had spoken to

5

some people, she had seen some people. But she also thought about how tomorrow she would have to begin again, invent something else . . . invent something else—she knew all too well—and how it was difficult, each day more difficult, she knew all too well.

THE SEVERED HAND

The pharmacist stared intently at his customer's hand and grew pensive, very pensive. He had never seen anything like it. The round hand before him was as thick as one of those balloons that children hold on a string in public parks. Once his astonishment had passed, he had to admit that this hand was rather pleasant to look at; although not classic in appearance, it had a certain beauty.

That said, the pharmacist and his customer were in agreement that it was important not to be influenced by aesthetic considerations, but instead to view the situation coldly, from a practical point of view: as such, this hand was useless. With no fingers and no joints, it couldn't grip; its large size encumbered its possessor and rendered life difficult for him. So, what more reasonable and sensible approach than to cut it off, utterly and simply? This idea, joyously suggested by the pharmacist, excited the customer, who had never imagined such a solution, likely due to a lack of imagination. Without waiting another moment, the pharmacist grabbed a small saw that was just within reach and merrily went about his work. Handled with caution, the saw gently shredded the flesh with its small pointed teeth. The minuscule tool made long work of it. After a few hours, the two men finally had the satisfaction of seeing one small part of the hand detach from the arm.

During the operation, the pharmacist ensured that the blood dripping from the hand didn't stain the customer's suit. But he couldn't stop a few splashes from spurting onto the patient's face. All this work had begun in the utmost gaiety. The two of them had taken turns recounting anecdotes from their personal lives, their childhoods, their teenage years, etcetera, until the moment when the pharmacist noticed that he had been the only one speaking for some time, while the other man remained silent. Lifting his eyes, he glanced at the patient; his face was pale, still, so still that it seemed drained of life; his absent gaze held a surprising resolve.

This attitude displeased the pharmacist. His ego was wounded: that the patient was putting on airs, that he was affecting a detached and distant comportment, as though "out of it," as though it weren't his own hand, really it was all very disagreeable to the pharmacist, who interpreted it as a lack of courtesy and deference toward him. Furious and aghast, he resumed his work, but his heart was no longer in it. This hand was beginning to repulse him, and he no longer derived any satisfaction from the way the saw attacked the bones. What a mess! A real carnage, a butcher's work! The flesh lent itself poorly to the saw, it shredded in small pieces and hung in strips. It was sickening! The pharmacist felt a wave of nausea rise in him. Once more he lifted his eyes to the patient and, suddenly, he understood. He was being mocked! This man with the round hand was mocking him: although his face was just as pale, just as still as earlier (perhaps petrified), it was impossible for the pharmacist not to notice a new development: a smile, a tiny little smile forming at the corners of the patient's lips. It was contemptuous, obsequious, even aggressive; an insulting smile. Yes, that was it, an insulting smile.

Mad with rage, the pharmacist brusquely dropped the hand that was now dangling from the arm by just a few strips of flesh. The customer tried to cushion the blow, but it all happened too quickly; his mouth contorted with suffering.

The pharmacist stood up, paced about his store without seeming to notice the crowd of people who had been waiting for a long time to be served. Abruptly he decided: since the man was acting like this, he needed to get it over with as quickly as possible. Gingerly approaching the patient, he grabbed the twitching hand and yanked it clean off with a vigorous tug. The detached hand was now between the two fat paws of the pharmacist, who turned it around and around several times; then, after amusing himself for a few moments throwing it in the air like a balloon, he suddenly became embarrassed. Negligently, he threw it in the trash after unhooking the wristwatch from around the jagged, bloody wrist. The patient, although still in a bad way, deemed the outcome of the affair a success. He could never have hoped for such a rapid solution to his woes. With a grateful smile, he tried to thank the pharmacist; but the pharmacist, still furious, paid no attention to this show of kindness, and it was only through a modicum of professionalism that he told the invalid, before pushing him out the door, to keep his arm elevated to help circulate the blood. The unhappy man wished he could apologize, for he saw that he had unwittingly offended this noble gentleman;

however, throughout the entire operation, he had taken pains to conceal even the slightest reaction out of respect for the learned man. At the moment when the pain was at its most extreme, the suffering at its most violent, with extraordinary effort he had managed to smile at the pharmacist. It was at that precise moment, he remembered, that the pharmacist had started to behave strangely.

As he was exiting the pharmacy, if they had left things on good terms, the customer would have happily asked the pharmacist permission to grab his hand from the trash—although he didn't show it, he was nevertheless rather attached to it—but the shame of having angered a man as remarkable as the pharmacist made him stammer a few timid "thank-yous" and tiptoe out the door, flustered.

Once outside, he was seized by the splendor of the summer day: the birds were singing and people were radiating happiness. Everything seemed delightful. He was happy, free, and amid this joy he decided to visit his friend Alfred.

At the bend in the road, the man saw a gathering on the main square. As he approached, he was surprised to see that every face bore an identical expression of hatred and rage. At the center of this infernal crowd, he saw only a bird, small, like all birds. He thought that this bird couldn't possibly be the object of so much hatred, but that in any case, it had better fly away (you never know what might happen in a frenzied crowd), and that provoking such a blood-thirsty group could only have unfortunate consequences. Since Hector didn't know what to do among these people, he left and carried on his way, liberated and radiant, to his friend Alfred's house.

Alfred lived in a tiny single room that was almost too small for two people. Hector liked the apartment, which gave him the impression of immensity, of air and space; he liked the skylight cut out in the ceiling through which you could see the moon and the sun, the sky and the stars. Hector also knew that his friend never felt the need to leave his home, that Alfred never went out. The shopkeepers sometimes spoke about it among themselves: two years since we last saw Monsieur Alfred! But no one was worried, for they were used to it. They simply wondered how he managed to live and feed himself.

Consumed by his thoughts, Hector continued his walk without noticing that night had fallen, a long time ago in fact, and that he was alone in the completely deserted streets. His memories brought him back to six or eight months ago when he'd last seen his friend, who had told him the story of Hop-o'-My-Thumb and had explained his inability, despite months of research, to draw the slightest conclusion. Spending even just two or three minutes at his friend's house did Hector a world of good.

Under an oppressive sun, Hector followed his path, taking care, nevertheless, to keep his arm in the air as the pharmacist had ordered. He regretted not being able to let it hang, because then the blood would pool on the ground rather than trickling down his arm. When the passersby saw his bloody stump, they mocked him and laughed idiotically as though it were grotesque.

Hector had now been walking for a full night and a full day, and he was surprised at not having already found his friend's house when it had only taken him a few minutes to reach it the last time. But he knew that these things happen and that it wasn't cause for concern. Despite great physical stamina, he felt exhausted, his limbs languid. He sped up, anxious to arrive. Finally, he saw Alfred's house. The key was in the door. Although he was a bit clumsy with his left hand, which he was not yet in the habit of using, he managed to turn the key and enter. He nearly cried out in shock: The room was empty. Alfred was not there!

Hardly able to believe it, Hector thought it must be a game and started to search for his friend. He moved all the furniture, looked high and low: but no Alfred! Suddenly, he noticed a hole dug into the floor at the far end of the room. He crouched down and saw a rope ladder hanging into the void. Total darkness. Carefully, he placed his feet on the rungs one after the other and started to descend. It was not as easy as he had first anticipated, for the space between the rungs was one and a half times Hector's height. And so in order to reach the next one, he had to hang by a single hand, gauge by sight the distance to the lower rung, then let go, jump to the next rung, grab on by his hand, hold tight, and so on . . . Hector was aware that a single misstep, a single blunder, would be fatal, would thrust him into the void with no recourse. He brought the greatest attention to the slightest gesture. Although courageous, after several hours of descent, he started to doubt the potential success of his undertaking. From time to time, he arrived at landings that led him through immense dark tunnels until he found another hole, another ladder; then his hope was renewed and he plunged once more into the void. Now the ladders were spiked with pointy nails that sliced into Hector's feet and hand; he suffered greatly, but not without feeling a sort of joy, for now more than ever, having reached the limits of his strength and his pain, he was certain that his undertaking was nearing its end. Sometimes he wondered whether it would have been more reasonable simply to wait for Alfred in his room (Alfred would certainly have returned), but he was ashamed of the thought.

Finally, he felt a firm and hard ground underfoot; he let go of the ladder and looked around. Here the darkness was so thick, the black so profound, that Hector had to close his eyes. It was only after great effort to acclimate that he managed to open them wide.

That's when he saw Alfred, Alfred who was shelling beans. Peacefully sitting on the ground, Alfred was shelling beans.

His friend's wisdom moved Hector, and he regretted neither the pain he had undergone to arrive, nor his detached hand, nor his bloody feet. He regretted nothing. Hector found Alfred changed. His friend had an immense beard and seemingly only one eye, but perhaps it was just a trick of the light. Hector sat down near the old man and helped him shell beans. Alfred, though silent, seemed very pleased by his friend's visit, and together they sang the songs of their childhood.

Having only one hand made the work difficult for Hector, and often he had to use his teeth; so he told Alfred the story of his severed hand, the pharmacist, etcetera. They laughed together, the two of them, happy to be reunited.

From time to time, Hector cooled down his swollen wounds with the shells of the beans, which had an extremely nurturing effect. The cave was cold and deathly humid. A rushing sound nearby led him to believe that there was a waterfall just a few steps away from where the two friends were shivering, bundled up in their clothes. The darkness rendered even heavier the presence of animals that Hector couldn't see but could hear whistling in his ears. Exhausted, he closed his eyes and dozed off for a moment. The cry of a child, of a baby to be exact, woke him with a start. When he expressed his alarm to his friend, Alfred reassured him by pointing at a bean shell in which an enormous baby was crying. The baby was so large and so tall that Hector thought at first that it had to be a dwarf. Alfred corrected him: it was definitely a baby, born not long before Hector's arrival. Alfred was in fact quite annoyed, for he had to notify the parents, but since he never went out, he didn't know anyone and had no clue who the parents might be.

The baby kept calling for its mother and cursing Alfred, as if he were to blame for the baby's birth. Hector was shocked that this vulgar baby was insulting his friend in this way, but Alfred told Hector he had to excuse him, for the baby must feel very alone. Being born without a mother must be a very cruel thing, and Alfred wondered whether the child would ever recover. Hector offered to set off with the baby to look for his parents, and Alfred accepted with relief.

To make his way out of the cave, Hector had to climb up the inside of a pipe that, although very narrow—hardly half the width of a man's body—was fortunately very long, about twenty yards, said Alfred. Hector, reassured, appreciated his friend's sense of organization all the more because he himself was completely lacking in it. He moved through the pipe with agility, accompanied by the baby. After climbing for several hours, pulling the child by the hair so as not to be separated from him, he couldn't help losing him at a bend in the pipe. Though he retraced his steps, he couldn't find the baby. With a heavy heart, he set out in search of the parents. He climbed for a long time before reaching an opening that he exited haphazardly.

Back outside, he was pleased to see a sky dotted with stars. He took a deep breath of the air that, although stale and slightly putrid, announced the coming spring. People on their knees were picking flowers from the side of the road. Cars passed at full speed without a care for the flowers and their admirers, which they flattened on their way. That's when Hector, to his great surprise, saw his little brother on the other side of the road. His hands were tied. Five police officers surrounded him, striking the child's body with a whip studded with skillfully scattered nails that ripped at his flesh. Hector would have liked to help his little brother, to comfort him, but he would have had to step over the cadavers strewn across the road to reach him, and Hector didn't have the heart. So he was forced to watch his brother's calvary from a distance.

Since the new laws had been voted in, Hector had known that his brother would be arrested; his natural kindness condemned him. Virtue and generosity were now punishable as crimes of public indecency. Anyone could denounce to the government those who brought shame to others and wounded their egos through noble and chivalric behavior. It was intolerable that a minority of people could claim to set the example and trouble people's consciences thus. That charade had gone on for too long, and now the government had taken extreme measures.

Hector had to toughen up no matter the cost. He had to vanquish his weaknesses, eradicate all humanity from his mind; in other words, force himself to be like other men: a good citizen.

He knew that his little brother's case would set a precedent, that the police, on his heels, would watch his every gesture, and that if he didn't show sufficient proof of his intentions, he would be done for!

Hector went into a bistro. The room was noisy and gay, the bar overflowing with people. He found a place in the middle of the crowd and ordered a drink. As he was bringing the glass to his lips, he noticed five police officers trying to hide behind a column. The moment had come for him to act. He had to prove the purity of his intentions in front of everyone—especially those five police officers. To miss such an opportunity could be fatal. The task was facilitated by his neighbor who had been amusing himself for some time now slashing up Hector's stump with a small knife he'd taken out of his pocket. In another time, Hector, who didn't like confrontation, would have patiently waited for him to settle down. If it had gone on too long, he would have politely asked the gentleman to stop his cruel game and that would have been the end of it. But now things were different, and with five police officers watching him, he had to act, and not be conciliatory under any circumstances. With great dexterity, Hector sank two fingers into his neighbor's eyes. Without having time to respond or to realize what was happening, the other man found himself sprawled on the ground in total darkness. Applause rang out. Hector waved to the crowd and, his conscience eased, looked the officers straight in the eyes. The man groaned and complained of a terrible burning sensation. A well-intentioned neighbor delicately spilled a few drops of eau de vie into his bleeding eyeballs. The wounded man let out a long scream, convulsed, and then froze in complete stillness. An ambulance driver who was already there picked up the body, placed him on a stretcher, and, with Hector's help, left the bistro. The two of them headed for the ambulance waiting out front (now there were always ambulances waiting outside bistros) and hoisted the stretcher into the car. That's when Hector saw the baby pass on the back of a large horse galloping at full speed. He was afraid the baby would fall. Eight days old was rather young for such exercise, but the infant seemed very relaxed and, recognizing Hector, laughed with his toothless mouth. Hector smiled at the child and made his way cheerfully through the town.

In the middle of the road, he noticed a woman draped in large black veils mounted on a mule. She signaled for him to approach.

Despite the large glasses that obscured the woman's eyes, Hector saw a deep sadness in her gaze. She had a beauty mark in the inner corner of her left eye, fat as a grape seed, which gave her face an indefinable charm. That beauty mark showed Hector that this was the mother of the baby, for the baby had the same mark in its right eye. Joyously he announced the birth of the child and offered to go with the woman to look for the baby. She didn't respond, but looked at Hector with eyes full of tears. Then, brusquely, she kicked the stomach of the animal with her pointed heels three times and it took off at a frantic gallop. During their conversation, Hector had mindlessly slid his hand into the stirrup. The suddenness of the departure took him by surprise. He couldn't withdraw his hand, stuck between the heel and the stirrup, and he was dragged, stomach along the ground, at the mule's side. He implored the woman to slow her course, but she was sobbing, sad and rigid. Her sadness was so painful for Hector to see that, now very emotional, he withdrew his complaints and settled for avoiding the sharp rocks that tore his skin, trying to straighten his head to keep it from bouncing too brutally on the hard ground. He was distracted from this venture by a new pain: for a little while now, or perhaps longer, the woman's pointed heel had been hammering Hector's hand, piercing it all over. The woman seemed to derive great pleasure from this. Leaning over to get a better look at her heel's handiwork, she purposely jabbed with her pretty little pointed heel where the wounds were fresh. Hector, his back broken and his body bruised, wondered how much longer this would go on. He was lost in thought when he saw his friend Alfred blocking the lady's path and brandishing the baby. The woman stopped short, took the child in her arms, and gave him her breast.

Hector thought of his own mother and remembered it was lunch time. The whole family would be waiting to eat at the table like every day. He would be late for the first time. He reproached himself for his negligence, all the more so because he hadn't been back to his parents' house for a long time.

He was slightly afraid to face his mother, whom he hadn't seen since the incident with his little brother and who must be in a dreadful state. He sped up. After hours and hours of walking, he finally arrived at the house. Entering the kitchen, he saw his mother pulling out her hairs one by one. Her mouth contorted into a wicked smile; she watched her son approach and violently pushed him away when he tried to get near her. She spoke hurtful words, exclaiming that she wanted nothing more to do with him, that he was truly his brother's brother, that he would surely send her to the guillotine if she didn't look out, that already at the market they had pointed a finger at her and although she had cut it off on her way and the crowd had applauded, she knew it would not suffice and that they would ask more of her, always more. It wasn't that she objected to the demand: a finger was nothing for her! She had seen worse things in her life! But the fact that she was now obligated vexed her, and at her age! Hector wished he could reassure her, explain to her that he had done what was necessary— and in front of five police officers—to align himself with the government, and so she had nothing to fear. But, full of rage, she wouldn't let him get a word in, continuing to groan and lament her fate. Finally, with a grand and noble gesture, she chased her son away.

Hector left the house with a heavy heart. Outside, he panicked at the sight of the teeming, gesticulating crowd moving in every direction on the sidewalk; the racket made by the ambulances, which were now speeding by continuously, one after another, overwhelmed him. Distraught, he was wandering through the streets when suddenly he remembered Alfred: there were still beans to shell and surely Alfred would be happy if he went back to lend him a hand. This thought comforted him and he continued on his way full of hope.

THE HEADLESS MAN

The woman took a seat on the bench. She was wearing a little black dress and a coat that was also black, brightened up with a pale blue scarf around her neck. Long blond hair framed her rather beautiful face, which her eyes, drowned in dream, bestowed with a unique absence.

The traffic on the street, the honking of cars, the sound of engines, the nearby entrance of the metro, into which numerous travelers plunged—nothing could wrest her from her reverie.

She shivered. She stared with amazement, then insistence, at the people strolling on the sidewalk; but her curiosity soon tired and she instead fixed her gaze in front of her, where she saw "Hôtel d'Angleterre." Surprised that she had never noticed this place, she stood up from the bench, headed toward the hotel, and entered. Men and women circulated through the lobby, smoking and chatting, while others read newspapers, sunk deep into armchairs. Standing in the middle of the lobby, she watched the comings and goings of these people with amusement. Suddenly she had the impression that everyone around her was giving her a strange look. Disconcerted, she remained still for a moment without knowing what to do. Then, determined, she walked toward the reception desk and asked the man standing there for a room. As the employee answered her, the woman noticed he was wearing a wax mask over his face. Intrigued, and hoping to animate the mask, the woman repeated her question and again requested a room. "I just asked you, for how many nights." The harshness of his voice made the woman jump. Realizing her response would determine whether or not this man would call security to escort her out, she said in a soft and conciliatory voice that the number of nights was up to him. Absolutely. In order to break the worrying silence that followed this response, the woman idly took a book out of her pocket and pretended to read it as she anxiously awaited what would happen next. Although she wasn't certain, she thought the man had just shrugged his shoulders, but perhaps he had just waved away a fly; so many had appeared around him in the last few minutes; nevertheless, unsure of the man's gesture, she decided the best thing would be to flee as quickly as possible. So as not to arouse suspicion, she kept the book open for a minute; then, taking advantage of the employee's momentary distraction, she turned brusquely on her heels and ran out of the hotel.

At the sight of her bench, still there waiting for her, she felt rather emotional and sat back down to resume her favorite pastime: people watching. The precision with which these people moved always amazed her. The way they chose to take one street rather than another, to turn right instead of left without a shadow of hesitation, delighted her when it didn't frighten her. However, for the past few days she had witnessed a curious phenomenon:

the passersby, at least some passersby, transformed abruptly, right before her eyes, into monstrous, nearly grotesque animals. Like that gentleman yesterday, who had transformed into a snake with an ostrich head as he lit his cigarette. In the moment, she had nearly screamed, but seeing that man, or that beast, undulate and crawl at the feet of all those people while they continued on their way, acting as though nothing was amiss, had seemed to her so ridiculous a spectacle that she ended up bursting into laughter. Later, a very haughty, elegant woman had turned into a gorilla on the arms of the man who accompanied her. He hadn't flinched.

She wondered, suddenly worried, what would become of those poor animals; a service order should be mandated to rid the streets of them, at night, in secret. She suddenly understood why in certain large cities there are zoos where they coop up rather curious beasts, and who all those people were who went to see them: parents . . . relatives . . . friends.

She was lost in thought when suddenly she noticed, mixed into the crowd, THE HEADLESS MAN. Her heart thudded in her chest. Her small face became grave and anxious. But once the man approached and sat on the bench next to her per usual, her anxiety gave way to immense joy.

The first time she had seen him, walking with no head among the crowd, she hadn't felt anything but pity for him, thinking it must be difficult to live in such a way; but when he had come to sit near her, as he did again today, she discovered that although he had no head, he did have a face: this face was impalpable like haze, mysterious like night; a face of shadow and fog, of light and poetry; a face

27

that stirred something deep within her and unsettled her very soul.

Since that encounter, which had taken place months ago, years perhaps, he had returned each day to sit next to her on the bench for a while. She didn't remember ever speaking to him. Once, she had almost asked him about his head, but not wanting to embarrass him, she had kept quiet.

She was staring at her friend's face, her eyes filled with wonder, when suddenly she heard something like a ripple of anger move through the crowd. Men and women, lined up on the road, were yelling incomprehensible words. She was afraid: afraid for her friend, afraid that these furious people would lash out at the headless man and cause him pain. Already she was picturing him ridiculed, lynched by them. But she would protect him from that mob. She would save him. She would lead him through radiant streets where daisies grow. Together they would jump over streams; hand in hand they would wander through fields and prairies while singing a Sunday song.

Finally she dared to speak to him and whispered, "Would you like to leave with me? I'll protect you . . . I love you so much!"

But she didn't hear the man's response; she'd had to expend so much effort to follow and guide her thoughts that now, exhausted, she neither saw nor heard a thing.

With utter sweetness, the man placed the woman's head against his shoulder and tenderly caressed her small face for a long time.

The woman broke away from the man's shoulder. She had the vague feeling that something important had occurred, but she didn't know what. She stood up, put on her coat, resumed her place, then remained immobile, absent, distant, until the moment when abruptly she remembered something she had to do and worriedly asked him for the time. The man looked at his watch and told her it was 5:30 p.m.

"Are you sure, monsieur?"

When the man gently repeated that it was 5:30 p.m., the woman murmured as though to herself, "How dreadful, I must have missed my train again. Do you understand, monsieur," she continued in a sad and weary voice after a brief silence, "for five years I've been trying to catch my train and I've never been able to manage it: a sick dog, a baby abandoned in a stream, a flattened cow dying on the road, so many obstacles have stopped me from taking my train. Before these obstacles, there were others . . . always others, and today I simply forgot . . ." Confronted with her implacable fate, the woman was now crying noiselessly; long tears slid down her pale face.

Distraught, the man tried to reassure her that she would catch her train if she allowed him to assist her, that by combining their efforts and establishing a strict schedule, he was convinced they would achieve her goal. Met with the woman's silence, his heart gripped with emotion, he repeated, like a prayer, "Allow me to help. I beg of you." The woman lifted her eyes to the man and saw the face of shadow and fog that she loved so much, the face of her friend, and murmured, "Come on. Let's go."

Together they stood and walked hand in hand through the now deserted streets and boulevards. Matching the woman's pace and letting himself be led by her, the man kept quiet. He knew too well that a gesture, a word, could break the spell and separate them again, perhaps forever.

When they reached the countryside, night had already fallen. A few cows were grazing tranquilly in the fields and raised their heads as they passed. The woman caressed one while telling it a thousand sweet words, then, followed by her companion, she entered a small forest. The man walked ahead of her and parted the brambles on the path, holding back the branches so that she passed without being grazed, and she advanced timidly, happy to be free and to be sharing with her friend this life that she loved.

At the exit of the woods, she clapped her hands cheerfully at the sight of a barn in the middle of the field. Lacing her arm through her companion's, she steered them toward it. The barn was filled with hay; the woman let herself fall into it as onto a bed.

Then, with great tenderness, the man covered the woman's body with his coat, still warm with his own heat. She looked at him and smiled. So much love passed in that smile that there was no more room in the man's heart for distress and despair, only for immense joy.

When she awoke with a start in the night, she thought she'd heard a noise near the barn; frightened, she looked around for her friend, and when she saw him she nearly screamed in horror. The man now had a head, a real one, with a very beautiful face. Frozen with terror, she couldn't wrest her eyes from that face, crazed at the thought that her friend, he, her friend, the man she had taken for her friend, was part of the world of THE OTHERS, that hostile, bizarre world of which she knew nothing except that it could not be her own. A somber despair took hold of her. Choking on her tears, she left, staggering from the barn.

The night was serene, and the round moon tenderly lit up the prairie. But the woman saw nothing. She ran, ran until she was out of breath, brushing aside the shadows that sometimes stood before her to block her path. Crazed like a deer hunted by a pack of wolves, she fell, got back up, resumed her demented race, disoriented by panic and grief. She crossed the prairie, the forest, ran along the river . . .

Then the man heard a harrowing cry in his sleep. Searching for his companion but not seeing her, he was seized by a strange, tragic fear; he left the barn and called for the woman. It was silent except for birdsong announcing the dawn. Then, crossing the field, the little wood, the prairie, he walked along the river.

And the man stopped short.

She was there, splayed on the riverbank.

He didn't fully believe it until, face pressed against her chest, he couldn't hear her heart beating anymore.

With the tender precautions one takes so as not to wake a small sleeping child while carrying them to bed, the man lifted the dead woman's body and, holding her against him, covered her face with tears and kisses.

One last time he looked at her innocent forehead, so moving, the naive and soft mouth that death rendered nearly childlike. He remembered her a few years earlier, running in her wedding dress through the wild grass. Grave and laughing, tender and anxious, there had been an uncertain flicker in her gaze . . .

Before throwing himself into the river, his wife's body wrapped around his own, he murmured to her as if she could still hear him, "My love . . . my Nathalie . . . I loved you so much."

COME

Today I'm finally starting on the goal I've set for myself: to write down the things that happen to me in a diary so I can have an exact record of them later on. This will also allow me to impose a bit of order on my thoughts.

Today, it's August 15. I'm sitting in the station waiting for the train that will take me to a country I know nothing about but that, if my intuition is right, should be extremely beautiful.

There's litter all over the ground and on a bench a man is splayed, reading a newspaper that's so torn up he is holding only a tiny shred in his hand. Poor thing!

I'll have to keep this brief because I think my train is about to arrive.

I feel too sluggish to imbue my notes with the necessary details. The countryside unfurls behind an opaque haze.

The veil that masked the houses and the land has ripped open this morning. Everything around me is remarkable. My eyes fill up with beauty.

B. told me he'd be waiting for me when the train arrived.

Without any stops, cities are succeeded by other cities, days by nights. Sometimes I have a hard time keeping my eyes open. When will I arrive there, where B. is waiting for me, and where they say it's nice to live? A piercing whistle and the abrupt halt of the train signal that we must have arrived. Fortunately all I have with me is a toothbrush and a comb, because I'm exhausted.

Maybe there's a strike going on because my train still hasn't come. I'm holding a leaflet of all the best hotels in the city. I'm enticed by one in particular. Apparently the bedrooms are superb and there's even a kitchen (in each room). I'd be able to prepare my own meals. I am in fact very hungry and a bit of bacon and some shrimp would be quite satisfying. But what if the train came while I was eating!

I wonder why all these people are walking around here, in this station, as if it were a place to take a stroll. They look bizarre with their heads perched on their necks, turning in every direction as if to see in front and behind at the same time. Maybe they know they're being watched? hunted? followed? and they don't want to be taken by surprise? They need to go elsewhere. Peacefully elsewhere. Then I'd be alone.

Since he said to me: COME! I'm surprised B. still isn't here. Maybe I'll find him in town.

The streets are hot and full of color. The sidewalks are painted red, burnt sienna, yellow, and sometimes royal blue. We slide through these streets as though on a rug.

It's practical, but after some time a bit monotone. Ten days of it would be too much in my opinion. Where is that hotel they said had such superb rooms with kitchenettes?

No one can help me: we don't speak the same language. So I'll have to figure it out on my own. Fortunately I have this diary in which I'm recording EVERYTHING! The fine dust in my eyes is blurring my vision and making things difficult, otherwise I'd already be in the hotel by now. I'm sure of it.

The city has a strange allure, with its houses that come up to your knees and its chimneys that climb to the sky. Maybe that's why there are so many people outside: they must get tired of it, of being inside. I think to myself that if I just walked into one of these houses I could finally splay out and get some good sleep. It's tiring, after a while, always keeping your eyes open!

When night falls, the sky glimmers with a thousand lights. They're blue, yellow, green, gray. Sometimes: lilac. There must be a celebration going on somewhere. I'm hungry, but I'm saving the hazelnuts in my pocket for B. He loves hazelnuts. I hope he still has teeth. At least one. Last time, he didn't have any at all. I still have all of mine; they're violet-colored. If I weren't writing in this diary, I'm certain that all these memories would be lost forever. One can never be too careful!

I'll try to recount everything. Everything that's important. Just now I went into the hotel. It's right outside the city and stands all alone in the middle of a forest. I happened upon it by accident. I had to go down a dizzying number of stairs. A little man with a large hump in his back appeared in the darkness and welcomed me very politely and courteously. His hair was red, blood-red, but his face was very pale. His bright, sea-colored eyes were glassy. I asked if he had a room for me; he answered that he was sorry but he had rooms only for himself; he liked to change rooms every night, and sometimes several times per night, which meant he couldn't spare any rooms for customers. His voice was shrill, his forehead imposing and protruding. When he walked me out, I noticed a few tears shining in his eyes.

Ever since, I've been obsessed by the image of that little hunchback: I wonder whether it might have been B. Several signs point to yes; most of all, that characteristic way he has of occasionally letting the lid fall slowly over his eye made me half-certain, but with this dust in my eyes, I can't say for sure. If it had been him, he would have recognized me. But maybe he preferred to act as if it weren't me. He's done something similar once before. I was in front of him and he acted as if it weren't me who was there but someone else. It was awful! Such panic to no longer know, suddenly. It's startling.

In the city today, people are raging like dogs: they drool, they yell, some shoot at you with a rifle, and others run all around the city naked and bloody. I wonder whether I'll stay in this country; it doesn't much suit me. What's important is to travel. It clears the mind, otherwise we'd go mad! That's what I used to say to B., but he never really seemed to understand me. He'd respond, "But that's all we do, my angel, we are indeed always leaving . . . leaving . . ." Meanwhile we stayed forever in the same place, in that hole he'd dug in the middle of a desert. Before us and all around us: the infinite. Talk about vertigo!

The air, the atmosphere maybe, I don't know, but a yell, some such thing makes me jump. I cough my lungs out. My hands and feet are ice. If I try to recall B.'s face or his presence near me, a great emptiness forms in my head. The only thing I can cling to: that COME from B. But I could have been mistaken about the city, the place, the country even.

The gentleman splayed on the bench came to sit next to me. He asked me what I was doing: "What are you doing here, in this station, sitting on this bench?" The kind of question I find unbearable. I said to him, "The kind of question I find unbearable, monsieur. Can't you see that such a question is disconcerting for me and useless for you?" I don't think I'll ever grow used to their way of being and thinking. It's best that I go. Elsewhere. No matter where; no matter where as long as it's where B. is waiting for me.

Moving endlessly through this hostile and inhospitable city saddens my soul. I prefer the sea. Especially the beach when it's covered in violets, then I lie down in the middle and my wait for B., little by little, fades away. The fish come to eat from my hand. Everything is silent and pink, and clouds of dead leaves flutter over the sea. There is never anyone but me on that beach when I'm there. Never anyone else at all.

Before I head back, I'll return to that hotel where the rooms are supposedly splendid and fresh as dew. And as for the little hunchback, I have to be sure one way or another. He's been waiting for me on the doorstep. "I've been waiting for you on the doorstep," he says to me. "Please be so kind as to enter." He opens a door. I go down a long staircase. I end up in an immense, bare basement. Empty walls frame the room. After walking around the perimeter many times, I realize that in one of the walls there's a door; it's very low. I open it and crouch down to pass through. It opens onto another staircase, this one very steep, very narrow, and hemmed in by two brick walls. It's very dark.

The cold is glacial. I go down and down and down. Another room. As in the previous room, the walls are bare; there are a lot of walls. Quite a lot. One hundred perhaps, or one hundred and fifty, separated by small narrow corridors; some so narrow that I'm forced to turn sideways to walk through them. A knock. I notice a door and a key in the lock. I say, "Who's there?" No response. Another knock. "I'm not going to open the door unless you tell me your name." A louder knock. I don't move. Fortunately the door is locked. The key gleams in the darkness. Suddenly I see, at eye level, a circle embedded in the door. It turns slowly, slowly. It pops out and falls to the ground. A hand and then an entire arm enters the hole. The hand feels for the key. The fingers graze it and, without turning it in the lock, grab it. The arm moves back toward the hole, slides through, and disappears. So, I have truly arrived! Now I'm certain that B. and the little hunchback are one and the same. Didn't he say to me earlier, "I've been waiting for you." And who other than B. could have said that?

This man is here next to me, still asking me the same question: "What are you always doing here in this station, sitting on this bench?" And what about him, always splayed or sitting next to me, would this man care to tell me what it is he's doing here?

UNTITLED

ISOLATED FRAGMENTS

The sun had not strained its silence and the sound answered the call of the flowers. A fire-red bird let out a harrowing cry; the woods vibrated in a long shiver and then silence settled in. A woman, a scarf on her head and a purse on her arm, leaned down and scooped up a dead bird in the middle of a bed of iron-gray ferns. She caressed the still-warm body, and the flame of her gaze brusquely crossed the attentive gaze of an owl.

There was a feral cry, and in the valley suddenly everything went quiet. The cows looked at each other, their eyes aghast, and the horses stamped and rolled around in the blood-red grass. The shepherd gave them a glass of milk to drink and, with his milky gaze, attentively examined the beasts that were writhing in pain and howling in distress. No one was there to rescue the shepherd's trembling soul. He lay down in the spiky grass that scratched his naked body and he smiled at the sky. But the sky that night was soulless. His eyelids closed; he saw a cross swaying and then, on the branch of a tree, a hanged body. The cows, motionless, watched the shepherd; the trees rustled with anger and all of nature rattled with sobs.

Nothing moved around him and the sky was steel. The man didn't understand. A glimmer in the distance. His heart began to thump in his chest. He tried to stand up, but his limbs were dead. A rooster started to crow, and the earth was moved by the dawn. The dawn said to the man, "Man, don't you see that the time has come, that there will be no tomorrow and that now you will meet your destiny?" The man looked at the voice. It was supple and undulating and fresh as dew. He replied, "You who know, will you tell me who I am?" It looked at him and with a silent smile gently closed his eyes.

NURSES

They slip noiselessly through the white hospital hallways, closing doors as they open others, holding syringes, vials, cotton, pushing rolling tables with rubberized wheels carrying iron tins, sharp or triangular objects, sometimes food, serum, blood, acid, sludge. Their faces impervious, impenetrable, impassive. Their gestures punctual, precise, methodical to the point of madness.

THE CADAVER AND THE CLOCK

A small golden chain, around her neck, disappeared into her blouse. I tugged on it gently; a round clock hung from it, continuing merrily on its way, punctuating living time with each second.

44

The night is ink; the sky shadow. The birds have stopped singing. A blackbird on a branch dies. The black angels are no longer violent. The demon has entered during sleep. Tomorrow the sun will not rise.

THE OBJECTS MOVE

Searching her house for the amazingly agile objects that were forever moving around, she lost an infinite amount of time.

Despite the unusual places she would sometimes find them in, the objects didn't manifest any surprise and didn't give her any sort of sign, for example one of sympathy, or of complicity, which would have provided her with a certain comfort. To the contrary. Perfectly unassuming and affecting absolute immobility, the objects, through arrogance, humorlessness, and insolence, sought to confound her.

PANIC

I feel it rising in me. It creeps up and I know that any effort to stop it would be useless. I have to wait. It will entirely invade my heart, my soul, my head. It will dig hollows in me and I will lose my reason in them. The void will offer itself to my despair without greed until my annihilation is complete.

Crouched like an animal in its hole, I will remain still, immobile, crushed by the wait, not knowing whether the enemy will engulf me in shadow or if, left to occupy my house, it will choose to abandon me in order to liberate me at last.

She is seated on the bench. Her frail, meager body trembles with cold beneath her worn clothing. Walking would warm her up, but she is so weary!

"You seem quite cold, my poor lady," says the distinguished gentleman who has just stopped in front of her. "You should drink a nice hot toddy; that would do you good."

She looks at him with astonished eyes. "Yes, that would do you good," repeats the man, who is now rifling through the pockets of his large coat. The woman, a glimmer of hope in her gaze, smiles at him sweetly, while the man continues to rifle through his pocket.

He takes out a small key. After flashing a jovial smile at the woman, he turns around and sinks the key into the door of the large car that's parked along the sidewalk, just in front of the woman. The man gets in the car, lights a cigar, turns on the engine, takes off. The woman watches him for a long time, this man fleeing in his car.

LIBERTY

Like the prisoner from his dungeon, a certain star, one evening, slipped away from the sky. Tired of illuminating the night, it descended sharply from the infinite and vanished into the void.

"Make a wish," said the mother to the child.

Stunned and distraught by the fall of the shooting star, the child vaguely understood the price of freedom. Tears of rage rolled down his pale cheeks.

THE MEETING

He thought that maybe it would have been better for him not to go to this meeting. The bus had now left the city and was rushing recklessly down the steep mountain roads. Here and there, a few gaunt cows were grazing the soft grass. Again he thought that maybe it would have been better for him not to go to this meeting, and he racked his brain for a long time trying to think of what had convinced him to go. He didn't know the city he was on his way to, nor the person he was supposed to meet.

The bus, full of travelers, was moving at breakneck speed. The night, abruptly fallen, was so black that it was impossible for X to distinguish even the presence of his close neighbors, whom he had seen only a moment before in the light of day. With no star or moon, the night suddenly seemed full of threats. Lamenting that he was not sleepy, he decided he would smoke to kill time and took a pack of cigarettes from his pocket; realizing he had forgotten his lighter, he gently asked his neighbor to the right, then the one to the left, whether they had a light. They must have been asleep because they didn't answer him. Disappointed, X returned the pack to his pocket.

In the early morning, he was stunned to see that there

was no one left on the bus except for him and the driver, even though it had stopped only a single time. What had happened to the other travelers? Concerned, X got up to ask the bus driver. Once at his side, no matter how many times he repeated his question, raised his voice, even shouted, the man didn't seem to hear or even notice a presence near him; X concluded that the man was likely deaf and, faced with the uselessness of his efforts, returned to his seat and shut himself inside his thoughts, which took a rapid turn for the worse and soon absorbed him so intensely that when the bus stopped, he wouldn't have noticed if not for the violent strike on his shoulder. Under the wrathful eye of the driver, who was pointing at the exit, X stood up. Hardly had he placed a foot on the ground when the bus made a surprisingly fast U-turn and drove off in a cloud of dust. X watched it disappear with a sigh of relief.

From the small hill he had just climbed, X admired the city before his eyes: it was immense, immense and immobile; no traffic of any kind disturbed the tremendous silence. If he hadn't been afraid of arriving late to his meeting, X would have happily remained for hours contemplating the order and harmony that reigned over the city. But not wanting to keep anyone waiting, and sensing that he didn't have a minute to spare, he went back down the hill and immediately set out on his way.

He walked down an avenue bordered on either side by sumptuous palaces and magnificent buildings; their facades, constructed entirely from pink marble, projected richness and rare beauty; there were a significant number of windows, the lowest of which were about a dozen yards off the ground. One thing, however, disconcerted him:

none of these houses had a door, and X wondered how anyone was supposed to enter.

Since he'd been walking for a long time and hadn't yet encountered another living soul, X worried he wouldn't be able to find his way if he didn't come across someone who could help him; a clock showing it was eleven reassured him; it was ridiculous to think that at such a late morning hour everyone could still be asleep in their homes! At one moment or another, someone would have to leave their house, and then everything would come together. Walking aimlessly, X found himself on a street he had already taken several hours earlier. Here he was again. So he decided to jot down the street names in a notebook, which would spare him a great deal of fatigue and a significant loss of time. With the back of his sleeve, he wiped his face, which was covered in sweat, and regretted not bringing his handkerchief. In fact, he no longer had anything! His papers, his wallet, his keys, everything had disappeared! Only his notebook remained. But he realized suddenly that this notebook would not be of any use because he had nothing to write with.

The sight of the boulevard he turned onto, stretching endlessly, as far as the eye could see, apparently not intersecting with a single street, and of the sun setting like lead, crushing out the light, suddenly made him want to turn back. He was seized by a feeling of inhospitality, of desolation. But he continued walking straight ahead.

The persistent absence of people in the street, the silence that reigned over the city, was starting to worry him quite a bit. He told himself that maybe the inhabitants of this place were at a festival of some kind . . . That happens sometimes: people clear out of town to go to a special event, he shouldn't panic, but this didn't make him any less anxious. This meeting was really starting to irk him! One doesn't just abandon people like this, especially not in a foreign land! They ought to have provided him with a guide! This lack of courtesy on the part of the people he was supposed to meet was somewhat hurtful. Suddenly realizing the absurdity of his situation, X found himself embarrassed for the Other. He wanted to believe, nevertheless, that this person had his reasons and that if he could have acted differently, surely he would have done so.

Feeling something brush against the bottom of his leg, X looked down and saw a cat. It was small and skinny, so skinny and so small that he felt a profound pity for it. Moved, X gently caressed the animal; the small fearful body shivered beneath his hand. The cat's gaze was fixed on him and he thought he saw something like supplication . . . a glimmer of hope. The cat was hungry, it was dying, so X sadly extended his finger to it.

When X came back to, he realized he was on the ground, splayed out on the sidewalk. A violent pain in his hand evoked his encounter with the cat; it had disappeared. A vending machine affixed to the wall gave him hope that he, too, might eat; he jumped up. One of the rows—the others were empty—contained a roll wrapped in cellophane. Trying his luck, X pulled the lever; this triggered a noisy mechanism and the sandwich fell to the bottom. The bread was golden and warm; unwrapping it, X noticed a thick layer of cheese, nice and creamy, and recognized its aroma as Camembert. It was all so unexpected that X stared at the bread, wondering if it wasn't merely the trick of a dream. Then, finally bringing it to his mouth, he took a large bite. An immense disgust gripped his insides and he vomited on the spot. What he had just put in his mouth could not under any circumstances have been food. Furious, he could not hold back the continuous vomiting that had seized him.

Sadly, he continued on his way. He noticed that there were no more rich and sumptuous palaces around him, only old houses, dirty and dilapidated. They too were missing doors; black gaping holes stood in the place of windows. He had the feeling that thousands of hidden eyes were watching him, observing each of his gestures, reading each of his thoughts. To evade the fear he felt mounting in him, he screamed, cried out; it was his own name that he screamed loudly. At that very moment, and as if responding to a signal, a strange and long procession appeared about a hundred yards in front of him; it was a striking and strange gathering, and X couldn't tell whether they were human beings or they were . . . But he didn't dare finish his thought, so terrifying did it seem to him. Prey to so much raw emotion, he didn't know whether to turn his back to the group and flee, or, on the other hand, to try and catch up with them. In the end, he decided on the latter.

Although the procession seemed to be moving very slowly and X was running as fast as he could, it was impossible for him to approach them, or even to get within a few yards. Curiously, the distance between them always remained the same. The pursuit was exhausting; X, feeling quite weak, would have liked to rest for a few moments, but the idea that this group might have been tasked with bringing him to his meeting and that, if he stopped, he risked missing the only chance given to him, filled him with such anxiety that he forced himself to speed up instead. The shooting pains in his finger made him suffer cruelly. The thought came to mind that eventually he would need to take care of it to stop the spread of infection. A torrential rain pelted down onto the city; it formed a greasy mud on the ground, which stuck to his shoes and made his race all the more dreadful. His clothes, plastered to his body, were like an icy envelope. To convince himself that his meeting was real—after all, he wasn't in this city for nothing, and suddenly he felt a desperate need to be completely assured of this fact—he tried to figure out the circumstances that could have led to this meeting. In response to this investigation, his brain, abruptly drained of all thought, offered nothing but a blank space in which X couldn't grab hold of anything. When he stopped running, he saw the procession disappear in front of him, row by row, as if erased by an invisible hand, soon vanishing completely. At the same time, he heard the deafening sound of footsteps on the road, startlingly close and even, it seemed to X, gathering around him. Then there was silence. And, abruptly, night. X could no longer distinguish anything of the street he was standing on. He knew it was long and narrow, with horrible houses on either side.

Not letting himself devolve into panic, and resuming his route very slowly, as calmly as possible, seemed extremely important to X. But, first things first, he would bandage his hand; once stable, it would cause him less suffering. In any case, it was worth a try; so he tore off a piece of his shirt and made it into a dressing. Indeed, the pain eased. This sudden improvement seemed like a good omen. But he was stupefied when, after a few steps, his forehead crashed into a wall; and yet he was sure he hadn't seen any obstacle in front of him earlier, in the light of day; the proof was the procession he had been following. But perhaps he had walked toward the houses instead of toward the street, which would explain everything. He only had to distance himself a few steps from the edge to be parallel to the houses with the street in front of him once again. Although that seemed plausible to him, he wasn't at all convinced. Nevertheless, he put his plan into action. He was walking in the dark now, fearful, his arms extended in front of him, dreading an obstacle. In about twenty yards, thirty at most, his hands crashed into a coarse wall. *I got my directions mixed up again*, X thought to reassure himself and to deny the mounting evidence. Because he was surely lost, he would change strategy, and, in order to continue on his way and avoid the disagreeable surprise of encountering another wall, or a house, he didn't know what exactly, he would walk next to the wall while running his hand along it. That would allow him to avoid getting lost and to keep moving forward. Since it suddenly felt strangely heavy on his shoulders, X removed his jacket, mechanically, and, mechanically, hung it from a nail that his hand had just grazed. He wanted to re-tie his shoelaces, but he noticed that they were gone.

Now that he had been walking for hours, an infinite number of hours, and with his hand still touching the wall, he felt a secret satisfaction at the idea that the strategy he had come up with was in fact perfect. No obstacle would stand in his way anymore. However, he wished he knew how long night lasted in this country, then he might have felt some relief; he would have seen things from another angle, with less pessimism perhaps. He ran his hand along his forehead, softly, very softly, as if to erase his thoughts.

He must have lost a lot of weight for, in order to keep his pants up, he had to tie a large knot in their front. And his shoes were now much too big; he became aware of this fact. To keep them on any longer would only aggravate his feet; he had made so much effort to keep his feet inside that asking any more of them, X understood, would have been too much. So without leaning down, he simply stepped out of his shoes and abandoned them there on the spot. He possessed so little, so few things, that this abandonment made him rather sad. It was as if his house had suddenly been taken. He took off running.

His hand had just brushed something; it groped, felt around, then entered into a pocket; X, suddenly remembering his jacket, felt a surge of joy. He grabbed it from the hook in order to put it back on, but then, his arm in the air, he froze; his blood ran ice cold. He realized that he was caught in a circle, surrounded by a wall, and that instead of moving forward, he had only gone in a loop.

Annihilated, suddenly drained of all strength, X let himself slide against the wall and remained there with his back against it, seated on the ground. The shadows were unfathomable. He saw only black. Nothing but black. He had the impression that his head and his entire body were filling with black.

This meeting astonished him to no end, just as the Other's neglect was continuously surprising to him. Remembering his walk through the city where he hadn't encountered a single human being, he wondered whether the Other was the only inhabitant. That would mean he possessed a strange influence. This thought was a balm for his heart: if that were the case, a person of that caliber wouldn't grant him a meeting only to abandon him! It would make no sense! He simply had to wait, entrust himself to the Other, and take a moment to rest. X lay down on the ground.

As he was trying to fall asleep, he heard a voice murmur in his ear, "You must come . . . I'm waiting for you . . ." The tone was plaintive, begging. X sat up and searched the shadows. He wanted to speak; no sound came out of his throat. "We must meet . . . Come." The voice was no more than a whisper. X was suddenly distraught by the idea that the Other needed him, needed his help perhaps. He made up his mind immediately: he would do everything possible to answer this call! First, he needed to get out of here. Perhaps somewhere along the wall there was a hole, a hole big enough for him to pass through. He didn't see any other way to find out except to grope the surface of the wall, from its base all the way up to the highest point he could reach on tip toe, with his arms in the air. And on like that, for the entire way around.

It was very slow work: it lasted months, and yielded no result. So X decided to do a second loop along the surrounding wall. But this time, to reach even higher, he would climb on the rocks and nails; their presence in the wall had been revealed to him by all his painful groping, which had slashed his hands. These supports, because they were invisible and spaced out irregularly, demanded infinite time and patience from X simply to locate them. But the real difficulty was keeping his balance once he had found a nail and managed to hoist himself onto it. In the dark, seized by vertigo, he would often fall down and have to start all over.

For some time now, X had been plagued with obsessive ideas. The advantage of this was that his mind was occupied for weeks on end. The idea currently preoccupying him was about his pants. They were the only possession he had left, and he didn't want to lose them at any cost. When he realized he was in fact completely naked, he leaped panic-stricken from his perch and splayed on the ground, face in the mud. When he recovered from the vertigo that had caused the fall and wiped away the dirt stuck to his eyes and mouth, he set out looking for his pants. Applying a specific calculation he'd come up with, he walked back 1,252 steps, then he advanced 28 steps. Then, turning his body to the void, he counted another 50 steps. Stopping short, he turned left, and after 1,222 strides he reached the precise location where his pants should have been. The ordeal exhausted him, but it was the only distraction he allowed himself, once or twice a year.

He was stupefied to find that his pants weren't there! *They've stolen them from me*, he thought, perplexed. Nevertheless he deemed this judgment a bit rash, for, in the end, how could there be a thief here ... He decided to do a meticulous survey of the ground. His position: his knees on the ground and his hands in front of him, a respite from the debilitating position he was normally obligated to assume to complete his daily work; he could finally relax. When he felt the precious article of clothing in his hands, he nearly cried with joy! He put the pants on and was astonished, once more, by how little contact there was between his skin and the fabric; the pants were so loose they felt more like underwear: he couldn't believe it! Sadly, he returned to the wall; sadly, he grabbed a nail, climbed onto it, and resumed his task. But when he lifted his arms into the air, stretching his body as much as possible in order to reach the highest point on the wall, his pants immediately slid down his body and fell at his feet. Unable to jump from one point to another without losing or tearing his pants, he had to gather them constantly, hike them back up and knot them at the waist, which of course cost him an infinite amount of time.

The only hand he could use to slide endlessly over the wall—for the other was in a state of extreme rot—was considerably worn, the nerves almost raw. When a nail got stuck inside, X would faint. He reminded himself that as soon as his tenebrous exploration was over, he could finally allow his body to rest; stretched on the ground, he would hold himself in a sweet stillness that would make him forget his suffering; he would let himself go. Abruptly he remembered that he had a meeting.

"A meeting?" said a small mocking voice inside him.

"Precisely! A meeting!" X said aloud.

"And where might that be?" questioned the same small voice.

Suddenly gripped with a violent anger, X began to knock his head against the wall as tears of rage poured from his eyes. However, once he'd calmed down, he resumed his slow walk. His body glued to the wall, he advanced like an insect over rocks, from one nail to another, for days on end, his wide-open hand traversing the rough surface.

Soon, the goal of this groping was no longer clear to him. It all seemed to be utterly useless. How absurd to find oneself in such a situation! What must he have looked like, in the dark and flattened against the wall! Descending cautiously, he removed his pants, folded them up, placed them near him, sat on the ground, and resolved this time to stay put.

It was thanks to a moonlit night, while X was mindlessly playing with his feet, thanks to a very full moon located just over the wall, that he saw, thirty yards up from the ground: a hole. He felt a shiver of pleasure tinged with hope. He kept his eyes fixed on the opening, wondering how he would reach it. It seemed to him that the only possible solution would be to pull out a few nails from the wall to loosen the greatest possible number of stones which, piled one on top of the other, would reach the height of the opening.

In order to identify, in the darkness, the place at the bottom of the wall that corresponded vertically to the hole, X quickly placed his pants there. The moon had shifted; he was in the dark once again.

Thus began an incredible amount of work. He'd had the idea that this hole could have been a sign from the Other, and so X devoted himself unceremoniously to his labor. However, sometimes his meeting seemed strangely insignificant; he even thought that once out, he wouldn't go to it. But he knew that this was only a game on his part, and that he would go!

The rocks piled up slowly in the shape of a pyramid; when X estimated it was high enough, he began the long and painful ascent. How many times already had he climbed that heap of stones! When he reached the front of the hole a few days later, X was dismayed. He couldn't believe how narrow it was! Distraught, dumbfounded, X kept his eyes fixed on the opening. Although he had lost a considerable amount of weight, he couldn't imagine being able to pass through it!

Nevertheless, he attempted the impossible. He started with his head. This was the most difficult part. Extremely so. His body followed boldly, stretching in a disconcerting fashion as he passed through. On the outside, X saw a cord. Using it to slide down, X arrived at the bottom and sat on the ground facing the entrance of a tunnel. All around him a blazing sun flooded fields of flowers with a joyous light. Long fine grass swayed gently. He shivered with happiness at the sight. Although he could have admired the spectacle forever, he told himself that when he so desired, soon, in a moment, he would experience the sweet softness of the grass beneath his feet; he was already imagining how cool it would be on the burning wounds of his body when he lay down. But he didn't want to rupture the enchantment of such a spectacle before he'd truly exhausted it.

When he got up and walked toward the field, X was surprised to find that a post, a kind of signpost, was there, right next to him, where before there had been nothing; glancing at it, he was about to look away when he saw inscribed on the plaque: MEETING. An arrow showed the way: through the tunnel. Without glancing back at the fields and flowers, his heart choked, full of regret, X plunged into the tunnel.

The dampness inside was glacial; it penetrated his

bones and his teeth started to chatter. Feeling himself suddenly bitten cruelly on his hip, he yelped and searched for the wound with his hand; to his great displeasure, he found that his pants were gone! Where could he have lost them? On the surrounding wall, perhaps, when he had passed through the hole . . . All the efforts he had undertaken to preserve this meager article of clothing had proved useless, and X felt profound disappointment and sadness. Fate was too kind to him, truly! A burst of laughter made him jump. "Is someone there?" asked X, who couldn't see anything. Since no one answered, he asked again, in a rather feeble voice, "Is someone there?" His feet were suddenly covered in water; soon it was up to his hips, then his neck. He understood that now he had to swim.

Stroke by stroke, he advanced haphazardly as snippets of frantic voices rushed around him. Vociferations erupted, unintelligible but uniquely violent, then everything was calm again. X heard nothing else except for his own very short breathing and the sound of water. At a bend, he saw a cone of light in the distance. That must be the end of the tunnel. He was surprised that the question of whether he would ever emerge from this tunnel had never occurred to him. Where had this sudden indifference come from? He couldn't explain it and remained troubled by it. Suddenly his body scraped up against rocks. There was no more water. Trying to stand up but unable to, X decided to continue by crawling on his hands and knees.

At the end the tunnel, X propped himself up, lifted his head, and looked around. A woman, her body naked and seemingly ravaged by worms, was dragging a young child behind her, also naked. He seemed very tired. The woman pulled the child forward, but the little one's legs sagged with each step. Here and there, men and women appeared. Those with a face—which was rare—had astonishingly thin mouths and glassy eyes. They walked, each alone and as though unaware of the others. Many were making threatening gestures. No one said a word. "Obviously from one country to the next, people can't all be the same . . . many things are different . . . surprising . . ." X said with a somber stubbornness as he resumed his body's reptilian movements. "I myself . . . haven't I changed . . . does that mean . . ." He stopped short in front of a small street where rats were skittering in single file over the pavement. A long shiver ran through him. *Maybe they're not dangerous*, X thought, turning down the narrow alley. Immediately a few climbed over his back and dashed down again, while others, jumping onto his face, bit him on the nose and mouth; some were content to cling on. Seriously exasperated, X swore that, once the introductions had been made and he and the Other were, perhaps, seated in large armchairs sipping tea, he would demand an explanation. If the Other, looking down on him, refused, he would insist, discreetly but firmly, that the Other elucidate the things that were tormenting him. But X was sure deep down that such a conversation would be unnecessary, for the Other, from the first moment of their encounter, would be eager to clear up any misunderstandings.

He was about to tear a rat from his ear that was more burdensome than the others, scurrying over him in a manic fashion, when he saw the street suddenly expand into a vast avenue full of houses; they were exceptionally low to the ground; X thought that no man, nor even a tiny child, would be able to stand up in them; there was, however, something comforting about them; he couldn't explain what, but he was very moved.

A bright light, bursting from a house a few yards ahead, suddenly blinded him. This had to be the location of his meeting with the Stranger! He was paralyzed with happiness. It was not that he had doubted ever reaching it, but now that he had finally arrived, after so much difficulty and sadness, he felt nearly intoxicated.

The idea that he would present himself to the Other like this, crawling on the ground, was intolerable to him; so, managing with tremendous effort to stand up, his body contorted with suffering, he took the few steps that still separated him from the house.

This house, contrary to the others, was immensely tall and narrow. At the entrance was a metallic door. As X approached and was about to knock, it swung open.

X cried out in horror; his eyes haggard, wild with terror, he tried to recoil. A whirlwind of air wrapped around him, enveloping him like a shroud. He felt himself sucked in irresistibly. Once he had crossed the threshold, the door shut slowly behind him.

X knew he had arrived.

THE FATHER'S APARTMENT

Every time I decide to walk away from this task, he stands before me and says, his eyes full of sadness, "I beg of you, don't give up, soon you'll be able to reach the top." Today, once again, he's here, worried, awaiting my decision. "I beg of you," he insists, likely sensing that I'm prepared not to give in this time. The sadness of his voice hurts my heart. I know already that I've lost. I glance at the skyscraper, then at the ladder lying on the ground. I estimate that I still have to make about a thousand more rungs to complete my task. He waits. His presence leaves me cold. He waits. A tear falls from his eyes, a few tiny drops of blood pearl on his forehead. To be the cause of such pain overwhelms me. To rid him of it, I kneel down next to my ladder and get back to work with a heavy heart. Reassured, he disappears.

I don't understand this power he has over me. Sometimes when I happen to see him approaching from a distance, he seems feeble, abandoned.

If I try to think of the reasons that led me to accept his father's offer, which the son communicated to me, to give me the apartment on the top floor of this skyscraper, I can't come up with any that are legitimate. That the apartment is, according to this stranger, of an unrivaled magnificence and furnished specifically for me to feel at home there did not, I know, have any bearing on my decision. It was this young man's persistence that made me give in. For years I would often run into him, and he would always be uttering that same offer from his father. Each of my refusals plunged him into despair, and an expression of ever-increasing suffering would appear on his face.

Brain crushed by the weight of the years, it's possible that I'm no longer able to sanely judge these things.

I work like a maniac on the construction of my ladder; it's what will allow me to reach his father's apartment.

Isolated from others, I grow old in a solitude that suffocates me more each day. I feel no joy, but I am not hopeless. I still have hope, although it's vague, very hazy, very crazy perhaps, the hope of finally being able to rest between heaven and earth one day. This place is deserted, only the skyscrapers and the forest, no flowers in sight, not a single blade of green grass to distract my eyes from the gray stone and the black trees.

I fell the trees. I cut them into little sticks of equal length to be made into rungs that I add to the ladder one by one. But I need so many that sometimes I think I'll never reach the end. The meaning of this work and of my life in this place escape me sometimes so profoundly that thinking about it too much can drive me insane.

One day I was dragging a giant tree I had just felled when suddenly I felt a hand on my shoulder. I saw a horrible hairy old man smiling at me. A few steps farther back was the young man, standing with his head down. "My father," he says in a barely audible voice, gesturing respect-fully at the vile man. I don't know what idea I had in my head of this father, or if I even had one at all, but upon seeing him the ground gave way under me. I felt like the victim of a ghastly trick. As the son repeated, "My father," I was surprised to see the man throw himself at his son and barrage him with kicks and punches.

The young man took these blows in silence, his gaze absent. He staggered, then fell, his face against the ground. The old man lifted his son by the arms and disappeared, dragging him in his wake.

That scene caused me great despair, collapsed my entire being. That father, so unworthy of veneration and yet so venerated by his son, made me wonder if I was a pawn in some dark plot. With doubt gnawing at my heart, I remained lying on the ground near my ladder for days on end, annihilated. For whom, for what, had I fought?

Then in a sort of lethargy, in a nurturing numbness, I became ecstatic, my head empty with a sense of well-being.

The stranger returned. His pallor and his diminishing body immediately made me think he must be sick. His lips were moving and I saw that he wanted to speak, but no sound emerged from his throat; he must have been fright-ened, for he started to shiver and his eyes betrayed an infinite distress. I forgot my own grief at once, and with the vague idea that perhaps I could be of some help to him, I tried to stand up. I managed after considerable effort. Finally on my feet, I approached him. He recoiled brusquely.

His embarrassed, almost guilty demeanor made me realize that he must have felt slightly ashamed of his father's behavior. To put him at ease, for he inspired a profound pity in me, I decided to pretend that things were going just fine, and I told him that I had found his father absolutely remarkable. His face lit up.

"Why do you cause us so much harm?" he said in a muffled voice. "I ask you on my father's behalf, he's the one who sent me." Then after a moment, he added as though despite himself, "I beg of you, there is so little left for you to do to reach the apartment, your ladder is nearly finished now." His demand that I resume my task would have made me hate him if his weakness hadn't inspired such compassion and guilt. He was right. I had to finish. I had embarked on a completely absurd venture that was beyond my comprehension.

The spring, the summer, the fall have been gone for a long time now. I am completely bare; only the winter, rigorous, subsists. The rain, the wind, the gray pierce me to the bone. "You'll be warm, you'll feel good up there," he says to me sometimes. At this idea, I become obsessed with working nonstop night and day, day and night, although the physical and moral suffering assailing me never ceases.

Cutting down entire forests, I create new rungs with no rest so that this ladder will bring me to that famous apartment, described as unimaginably delightful. However, sometimes I'm struck by the lack of necessity of my life. Then I sink into despair for days at a time, prepared to die from it. But then he appears and looks at me with a long, sad gaze, and I'm gripped with remorse and self-reproach so immediate that I resume my labor.

Many months had passed when I saw the father again one day. His son wasn't there. Since my work was nearing its end, I thought maybe the old man had come to praise me for my dedication. Suddenly I had the idea that I should thank him for the apartment he was giving me. So I stammered a few clumsy phrases. Advancing toward me, he reached his hands out with a dignified gesture. They were long, slender, incomparably white. Thinking of mine, seeping with blood and pus, I knew I couldn't shake his hand under any circumstances. "You have one final task to complete. Then you will be able, without shame and as my equal, to leap into my arms." He disappeared without another word. I was horrified. Now I understood the abjection of this man, and just how insurmountable the distance between us was. The panic and distress I had managed to vanquish until then, one second at a time and at great cost, now constricted my heart, suffocated me, invaded my thoughts and my entire mind. I was no longer myself but an accumulation of panic. I was wallowing in it, bogged down in the hope that it would conquer my reason. Perfidious, it stuck to my skin. I was determined this time to abandon my final task: to position the ladder against the skyscraper and take possession of the apartment.

That's when he appeared.

We remained still for a moment, facing each other. Our eyes met and I knew that I would continue. He lowered his head, turned to leave, and vanished into the night.

I succeeded with incommensurable difficulty to hoist the ladder against the side of the skyscraper.

Bearing the weight of my suffering for long days in a row, I began the ascent. I had only a few rungs left to climb when I noticed, in the far distance, like two dark specks on the ground, the father and his son.

Their unexpected presence suddenly filled me with immense happiness.

I was about to climb through the window and enter the apartment, of which I could see nothing beyond the encompassing darkness, when, brusquely, I felt the ladder detach from the wall. Frightened, I looked down. The old man, his two hands gripping the sides, was pulling it toward him. Once it was vertical, he held it steady in that position for an excessive amount of time, which caused me great discomfort. Screaming with all my might, I demanded that the old man put the ladder back in position. I implored him, begged him. He did nothing. With each of my requests he shook the ladder and laughed like a madman. Mute with fear, I didn't utter another word and shifted my effort to clinging onto the rungs as tightly as I could. Suddenly he stopped. Taking advantage of that pause, I tried to descend; then he started to shake the ladder again with a crazed violence and his laugh carried all the way up to me. Perhaps I still had a chance: I would address the young man who was standing near his father with his head down. After a moment of hesitation—finally—he appealed to his father. By way of response, the old man kicked him in the stomach. The ladder was now leaning at a staggering slant. I was dizzy. Sweat dripped down my neck. The effort I made to keep my feet fastened to the ladder wore me out. Soon it was no longer possible. I lost my footing and my body dangled into the void, my arms stretched dangerously. The old man stopped once more. My arms were pulling so hard that I feared they would detach from my body. Then there was a back-and-forth movement so rapid and so violent that my body banged haphazardly against the rungs and was then again suspended over the void. I realized that this old man possessed a superhuman, diabolical strength and would never give in. My arms ached. Exhausted, I could no longer lift the arm I had let slide down my body. My hand, out of strength, lost its grip little by little, and I fell into the void as the old man burst into laughter.

I don't know where I am. The sun is gone. I'm walking along a path I can't see. The silence is absolute.

There's a bright spot in the distance. It seems to be the earth. I'm not sure. It might also be paradise—a place full of joy and frivolity inhabited by magnificent beings. They're called humans. Maybe if I walk long enough I'll reach them. Sometimes I pass a stranger on my path. I can only see his pale, sad face and his arm when he shows me the way to the bright spot. Without him I wouldn't have the strength to continue. I would let myself slip gently into the shadows. He's the one who told me that over there, that's the earth, and the earth is paradise.

Should I believe him?

I'll never reach it.

THE CAGE

There were days of fog, days of rain, and days of sun. Days of cold, days of wind, and more days of sun.

"What lovely weather!"

"What lovely sun!"

The entire town was vibrating with a joyous murmur.

"Yes, what lovely sun!"

"Really so lovely! And what weather!"

But she, she didn't really notice the color of the sky. Only when the women went out in the streets in dresses, the men without overcoats, and the terraces were filled with people, then she felt a bit more alone, a bit sadder, too. It wasn't until the rain, the wind, and the frost dismayed the passersby, who walked quickly without looking around, their heads tucked behind their coat collars, that she felt a certain harmony between the world, the weather, and herself: a harmony of grayness, a harmony of sadness.

The boulevard bathed in sun and the buds ready to burst announced that a brand-new spring had arrived. She was walking, or rather *strolling*, since that's the term one uses when out on a Sunday to get some fresh air in the streets, with no desire and no purpose in the middle of a radiant crowd. The windows that enticed the passersby left her indifferent; what pleasure could she find in a new bag, a ring, or a scarf? No, her concern was to figure out what she could do with her afternoon to fill it as best as possible. Since she had the good fortune that day, like every Sunday, not to be at the factory, she had to make the most of it—she was always saying this to herself: that she had to make the most of it. But she never knew how to go about it, and each Sunday found her a little more distraught, so she would go out, in the vague hope of finding outside a remedy to her turmoil.

As she passed by a movie theater, she read on the poster: MODERATO CANTABILE. Although she didn't understand the meaning of those two words, she found them lovely to read; to herself, to hear them, she said the words quietly, softly, and enjoyed repeating them to herself again. She was tempted to join the line of people waiting to see the film, but the risk of having to leave the theater during the screening, which often happened to her, ruffled by the presence of an elbow brushing against her breast or an unfamiliar hand wandering, as though by accident, over her knees, made her renounce the idea. So she resumed her stroll.

Already the day seemed interminable and she began to long for the end. And yet, during the week at the factory, the coming Sunday always seemed like a halo, like it would surely bring about some kind of joy, some great change to her life! Not wanting to give in to the discouragement that awaited her, she lifted her head, quickened her pace, and forced herself to smile as though she were happy. On the opposite sidewalk, she saw a circle of onlookers. Crossing the street, she headed toward the group, but the people in front of her hid the spectacle and she had to wait a long time to see that it was a monkey performing acrobatics. A man, strong in stature, was wearing faded velvet pants and a white grease-stained bathing suit. At his command, the monkey performed a handstand on the back of a metal chair, balanced on one hand, then leaped onto the shoulders of his master and ran his hands through the strands of his hair as though looking for lice. Then, pretending to find one, he squeezed two fingernails together as if to crush the louse to the great thrill of the audience, who chortled with laughter. Jumping to the ground, the monkey bowed, removed his beret from his head, and held it under the noses of the onlookers, who paid for their pleasure with a few coins.

She left the group vaguely nauseated by what she'd seen. Having felt that sensation a few months earlier, she felt the circumstances abruptly come back to her. It was a Sunday, she'd been at the zoo. From the beginning, the despondent state of the animals, contrasted with the gaiety of the people promenading before these prisons, had provoked a singular malaise; all those animals, sad and solitary behind their metal gates and exposed to the view of the onlookers, had provoked a feeling of shame in her; the animals that she knew to be the most noble, the most savage, seemed the most deprived of their dignity. The lion now appeared as an apathetic, gloomy animal. Nevertheless, it still possessed enough nobility to display, as a sign of scorn for the curious, an attitude of superb indifference; they took it as an insult, as evidenced by their words and their irritated expressions; those who believed themselves to be a coveted object for the KING of animals would have liked to see the big cat charge and pounce at the gate in the wild hope of harming them; they would have liked to see it fall back down and then charge again while they, mocking and superior, would laugh and sneer at the animal's vain efforts. Vexed to see that the lion not only had no desire for them but ignored them entirely, they masked their disappointment with a few derogatory remarks for the big cat and avenged themselves by running to see the monkeys. There, no coyness! No posturing! They were on equal footing and spent hours laughing at these animals as they aped the humans. She left the zoo very quickly and never returned.

People walked leisurely along the boulevard. The facial expressions of those couples, of those families she passed, gloomy and rigid, filled her with surprise; she imagined that if she had the chance to find herself on the arm of a loved one, she would have been resplendent with happiness. But perhaps they didn't love each other, or didn't love each other anymore? According to her coworkers at the factory, love wasn't essential for marriage. When she'd refused the marriage proposal from her supervisor because she felt for him only friendship and not love, everyone had said, "Love! Love! Get married first and after you'll see . . ." Perhaps that's what these people had done: they had married first and then, after, they had seen. Suddenly she felt extremely tired. Everything seemed drab, the street, the people, the houses; how ridiculous was that city of stone from which nature was excluded. Now she regretted having gone out. To kill some time, she went to sit on a café terrace; there were many cafés on the boulevard, all packed with people. She chose one at random and found an empty table in a corner after some searching. When the server asked what she wanted, she ordered a coffee; she adored coffee but drank it rarely; at night it kept her from sleeping; at the factory it was a vile concoction; and in the morning she was too tired to muster the strength to make herself a cup. One night, too tempted, she hadn't been able to resist the pleasure of drinking a cup and, racked with insomnia, she'd gone to buy a book at a newsstand. But, to enter thus into the life of two people who love each other—it was a romance—who live only through each other and for each other, had given her such a sharp awareness of her own solitude that she'd shut the book before finishing it and cried the rest of the night. Now she didn't let herself drink coffee except like this, on a Sunday afternoon.

It seemed urgent to leave, to avoid the trap into which, if she wasn't careful, her thoughts would inevitably lead her; better to mix into the crowd than to examine it from the outside with a critical eye. She thought about how she had another four hours to kill before going back home. Then her day off would be over.

Going from street to street, she arrived suddenly at a square where a festival was taking place. It was dripping with light and dark with people. In a din of shouts and music, children, men, and women on carousels screamed with fear, cried with joy. Others were watching, speechless, as their children spun around on the back of a swan, a pig, or a bicycle. She didn't know what to do: enter the festival, or continue her walk? Making up her mind, she joined the moving mass and passively followed its course. She observed the ghost train and the scenic railway, the bumper cars and the swings, carnival games and planes that launched into the sky and came back down in a nose-dive; she would have liked to ride in a plane, but to do it alone didn't really appeal. Around her people were calling out and laughing, eating marshmallows, cotton candy, gingerbread in the shape of a heart. Every face was beaming with joy.

Jostled, hurried, shunted around in the middle of the crowd, she no longer saw anything of the festival except the backs swaying before her. In an attempt to break free, she cleared a path through the crowd and arrived at a booth where a woman was inviting people to enter for a franc. Taking the coin out of her bag, she gave it to the cashier who showed her through a curtain, and she found herself in a vast room with walls covered in mirrors. She saw herself in turns as a dwarf, a giant, enormous, spindly, wider than she was tall, short-legged, face disfigured, hideous. Hearing the bursts of laughter erupting from everywhere, she imagined it must be funny to see yourself like this when you're with friends, but alone, it was more like a nightmare!

While she was looking at herself in a mirror whose deformation was particularly grotesque, an image materialized next to her own; its silhouette was so ridiculous that she turned her head, curious to judge for herself the true form of her neighbor. Their gazes met, locked. She had the dazzling sensation that this was for life. The same emotion rendered the two of them stunned and silent. The man approached her and, as naturally as if he had always known her, drew her into his arms and held her there, tenderly squeezed.

Then, together, they rode in the plane; together they ate fries and pralines. Together they walked through the festival, their hearts full of love and joy. He had asked her name. She had said, Berthe. And when he had repeated, Berthe, she'd had the impression that she was hearing her name for the first time. His name was Pierre, and in Berthe's heart, in letters of gold and fire, the name Pierre inscribed itself forevermore.

The bistro in which they had their first aperitif became their usual date spot. Gaston, the owner, with his cheerful eyes, his jovial air, and his way of always welcoming each person with a kind word, elicited an immediate fondness; his customers liked to come to his restaurant to unwind for a bit at the end of their day. For Pierre and Berthe it had become a ritual; they stayed there for a bit then they went back home. Cooking was a pleasure for them, to sit together at the table: an enchantment verging on a miracle.

The nights, tender and affectionate, profound and voluptuous, enclosed them in the mystery of love. In the morning each of them explained to the other how even in sleep they hadn't left the other. It was laughter and kisses; it was the mug of hot coffee Pierre brought to Berthe in bed; it was the joy of biting into the same slice of buttered bread. It was the amazement of finding themselves together. For them, a fairy had waved a magic wand and changed the world. But already they had to separate and that separation was a heartache. Kisses . . . another one . . . Just one more . . . the last one! And they would leave each other for the entire day!

One night when they were at Gaston's, Pierre suggested to Berthe that he bring her to the zoo the following Sunday. Had she already been? He had, often; he said it was a place he liked quite a bit and that it would make him happy to go with her. Berthe suddenly remembered her trip to the zoo and the unpleasant sensation she had felt; but with Pierre everything was so different . . .

When they were about to leave, having finished their drinks, Gaston offered them another round. Lately, he found himself truly disappointed when these two customers left the bar and the door closed behind them; he wanted to keep them, hold on to them for a little while. He had seen people, couples, lovers come and go in his bistro for forty years, but with these two, it wasn't like with the others. When he saw them arrive with their faces full of real happiness, their eyes flooded with the cheerful tenderness they shared, it made him as joyous as a child's laugh; a breath of fresh air entered his café; all at once he forgot his fatigue; the bottles flew in his hands; he experienced a new pleasure in serving his customers. He felt like a new man. Pierre and Berthe, after accepting Gaston's offer, after drinking and toasting and chatting with him, finally left the café.

Little pink, mauve, and blue clouds, as though painted by an artist to decorate the sky, slid slowly through space. The large, noisy crowd made the zoo seem like a fair. Berthe watched people eat voraciously at three in the afternoon, as though seeing the imprisoned creatures whetted their appetites, sandwiches, fruit, fries, chocolate bars. They also fed the animals, anything at all, trouser buttons, coins, an old car key, a pocketknife, really anything at all, just to see the expression the animals would make, their reaction. But they were usually disappointed, for the animal would gobble it down without offering any reaction. It wasn't until that night, or one or two days later, that that accumulation of various objects in its body would make the animal fall ill, sometimes fatally. But no one would be there anymore to see its suffering.

The two of them walked in silence. Pierre was surprised not to experience the same pleasure he had felt on previous visits walking through this zoo. A new sentiment of sadness on seeing these imprisoned animals spoiled his pleasure. He had never realized before today just how upsetting the condition of these creatures in their prison was. It was now unbearable to him.

They had already seen the stag and the doe, the elephant and the giraffe, the panther and the lion, when suddenly they noticed, enormous, coiled upon itself, a snake. On the sign was written: BOA. Berthe couldn't suppress a shiver as she watched the reptile slowly unfurl itself; the power unleashed by its body was terrifying, yet she couldn't look away; now it was slithering over the ground in a slow, undulating movement. In the snake's advance there was something invincible, as though nothing could stop it. It made a half circle with its body, then, soon, a complete circle, geometrically perfect. Then, no doubt satisfied, it remained still, its eyes closed.

Suddenly Berthe noticed that she had forgotten Pierre. The presence near her. Turning to him, she saw he was pale, immobile, staring at the snake. "Pierre!" she cried, forcing herself to dispel the emotion that had just overtaken her. "Pierre!" she repeated. "Pierre! Pierre! Tell me, what's the matter?" she asked, frightened to see him still frozen and staring at the boa. Pierre jumped and, as though speaking to himself, murmured in a whisper, "It's over . . . a horrible vision . . ." But his gaze remained riveted to the snake. Berthe placed her hand in Pierre's. "Let's go home, Pierre, okay?" she said, trying to lead him away from the boa. At the touch of that little hand he felt frozen in his, Pierre suddenly regained contact with reality and, tearing his gaze away from the snake and bringing it to Berthe, he thought he was dreaming her, her his love, her, his beloved Berthe, there, right next to him.

He didn't speak, nor did Berthe, of what had just happened. Pierre, because he was forcing himself to hide the inner tumult the boa had provoked in him. She, because she saw Pierre too preoccupied: from the start the snake had exerted a sort of fascination over him. Then a strange vision had appeared to him. As though through a light veil, he had seen Berthe alongside the boa. On her knees next to the snake, she had been caressing it sweetly, the expression in her gaze indescribable. A feeble smile had roamed over her lips. After an uncertain amount of time, just when it seemed she was about to speak, the image had suddenly vanished. He felt certain that something had just been uttered to him, and he had to find out what it was.

From then on, obsessed by the idea that the vision hid a secret, Pierre dragged Berthe to the zoo every Sunday; they no longer looked at the stag or the doe, not at the lion or the giraffe; Berthe's hand squeezed in his, Pierre raced down the paths, stopping only at the boa. Outside of the world and time, he would spend hours scrutinizing the animal's eyes.

Berthe didn't ask any questions. Berthe never asked questions. If Pierre had not yet explained the madness that drove him to the zoo each Sunday, it was, she was sure, because he could not. She herself said nothing about his unease, but the confrontation between Pierre and the snake, that moment of their encounter, incited a troubling state of anxiety and alarm. When she saw that the boa was unfurling its hard and smooth body in a silent slither, that suddenly it was lifting its head again and that it was staring in their direction with its small beady eyes, her blood ran cold, and she reached for Pierre's arm as a drowning person grasps at a life preserver. But Pierre didn't hear Berthe's silent call. Seized in a diabolic game against which all force was powerless, with the renewed image of Berthe near the boa, he was living a nightmare that he didn't have the strength to cut short through his own willpower. Berthe knew that she had to wait. Then, abruptly wrested from his contemplation, Pierre would turn to her, haggard, he would take her in his arms and hold her there tightly squeezed as if he wanted to protect her from some danger. He would caress her face, kiss her on the forehead, the eyes, the mouth, and she, in his arms, would forget her terror and distress. For a moment she would be reassured; happy.

The daily routine of their life continued on as in the past. Never did they reference the last Sunday nor the one to come. The mortal wait for the arrival of the fateful day turned their weeks into a burden that was all the heavier because they both wanted to conceal the weight from the other; it was the gift of love that they gave to each other each day.

At night they found themselves at Gaston's; it was a rite to which they adhered implicitly. The owner was sad to see their sullen expressions. She especially, who appeared thinner and had circles under her eyes, caused him concern. Tiny details more convincing to his eyes than those displayed by others in public proved to him that their love was intact. Hoping that if he knew their troubles he might be able to help, he often wanted to ask them questions, but his fear of being indiscreet held him back. So instead he offered them a small drink, like before, but now they typically refused his offer as though in a hurry to leave, and even more than their abbreviated presence, Gaston's sense that his two friends were unhappy caused him real sorrow.

That Sunday, Pierre didn't know how to explain why or through what miracle he felt, upon waking, RELEASED FROM THE BOA; but his liberation was complete: the boa no longer existed. To celebrate, Pierre longed for the noise of a brass band, the sound of a bugle, the delirium of a jubilant crowd . . . He sat laughing at the end of the bed; Berthe was still asleep. He was impatient for her to wake up. So impatient that, unable to control himself any longer, Pierre leaned over Berthe and gave her a long kiss; as soon as she opened her eyes, he yelled, "Do you see, Berthe? It's over! The boa! It's over!—over—over . . ." Now he was spinning around the bedroom, singing, "Over . . . Over . . . Over . . ." Then, turning back to her, he declared that they would go for lunch in the countryside. At an inn. Would she like that? Yes? Marvelous! And then they would go for a stroll through the forest. Taking her face in his hands, he asked if she could ever forgive him for those awful Sundays when he'd dragged her to the zoo. But, for some unknown reason, he didn't reveal to Berthe the motivation for his visits: the vision.

Berthe listened to Pierre speak while trying to understand why she felt outside of his joy when she should have felt it as intensely as him. Shattering her nights, worry had often left her awake until dawn; that night too she had slept just a few hours; her head was emptiness, chaos. Pierre, surprised that she wasn't saying anything, and noticing the pallor of her face, the dark circles under her eyes, was suddenly afraid that she might be ill: Would she rather stay at the house? Would she prefer, instead of going out, to stay in bed and rest? He would stay with her; he would take care of her; he would dote on her. At noon he would go out and buy groceries and bring her anything she desired for lunch. He—Berthe cut him off, laughing and jumping up from the bed, and threw herself into Pierre's arms.

She was angry with herself for having dampened even for a moment the joy of Pierre, of Pierre her love, of Pierre who was her breath; her life. She needed to vanquish that feeling of emptiness in her head and then for her, too, everything would be joyous.

The presence of a small invisible world that one could only perceive through subtle sounds filled the forest with mystery. Sensing with the wind that had just picked up that their death was near, the leaves trembled gently. A number of them were already flying, soaring, making the final voyage. Sitting on an embankment, Pierre and Berthe, heads raised, watched the leaves' trajectory. Sometimes in a surge of energy one would climb back toward the sky but, as if defeated by the effort, would sink back down just as quickly and land, dying, on the path.

The silence of the forest brought to life the tiniest noise; a slight snap, a rustling of leaves alerted the ear more than any earsplitting noise in the city. Beaming like two convalescents emerging fully healed from a nearly fatal illness, Pierre and Berthe saw life through an enthralled gaze; it was their possession, a treasure that henceforth they would know to safeguard from any violation. Together they made plans; Pierre told Berthe that she would no longer have to go to the factory, that they would have children. Three, said Berthe. Pierre said he'd like that, but on the condition that they all look like her, because she was beautiful with her long legs, her big sad eyes and her sand-colored hair; laughing, Berthe said that on the contrary she would ensure they were all made in his image, otherwise she would abandon them. Pierre also said that one day they would buy a little house and spend vacations there with the children, and Berthe listened rapturously to Pierre's words.

Pierre lovingly caressed Berthe's face resting on his shoulder; the certainty with which he felt that nothing would be able to distract him from her anymore and that their life would be proportional to their love filled him with a happy plenitude. The bus advanced slowly through the suburbs; it was the time when the pleasure that had inspired the motorists to leave the city for the countryside for an entire day was repaid, at night, by a return that demanded hours of patience and waiting. Some people, those whose fragile nerves suddenly cracked, would start to behave like lunatics, swerving abruptly from their lanes and deliberately passing to the left of the continuous line of cars while honking nonstop and hurling insults at the people they passed.

At the station, the passengers stood up and jostled each other toward the exit; in their wake as the last ones off, Pierre and Berthe stepped off of the bus.

There was a scream. There was a body that bounced, like a balloon, off the hood of a car. There was, on the sidewalk, in front of Berthe, the bloody and mutilated body of Pierre. Then there was, around her, a confused murmur of voices and the hazy vision of a gathering of people. In her head, a word echoed like a knell. And Berthe didn't know anything anymore.

Of what had been, of what was no more, Berthe didn't know anything anymore. She didn't suffer; she didn't think; it was a vertical drop into the void. As in the past, she continued to go to the factory each day. Automatic gestures learned from years of labor allowed her to complete her work. Her coworkers found her bizarre: she spoke to herself; sometimes they saw tears slide slowly down her cheeks although her face showed no emotion. Returning home at night, she set the table for two but ate off to the side, on a chair, nibbling a piece of bread, a bit of cheese, or a slice of ham. In the morning she awoke with her head reeling from nightmares that obliterated her.

Of Pierre, of his death, of their love, of their happiness: Berthe remembered nothing.

She awoke with a start, sat up on her bed, and looked around. It came from behind the door. Footsteps, strangely lead-footed, approached her bedroom. The door opened slowly. Enormous, hideous, an animal entered; other animals no less repugnant followed. She saw them advance toward her bed and then, encircling it, spin all around in a frenzied farandole. Frozen with terror, her body drenched in sweat, she didn't dare move and watched the monsters, some of which had only two enormous eyes for a face that were teeming with countless tiny worms writhing in every direction. Others had a dozen ears seemingly planted in their backs that continuously reached up to touch the ceiling and then slowly descended and disappeared into the animal's body. The monsters formed a moving mural around her that made her dizzy. Abruptly the animals froze; from their bodies came long human groans, the intermingling voices of men and women and children. The laments became more harrowing, the groans more desperate. To drown out these cries of intense distress, Berthe let out a long scream, then she lost consciousness.

Her nightly hallucinations enclosed Berthe in a horrific world from which she emerged in the morning haggard and dazed. Her coworkers worried about her: Why didn't she go see a doctor? She had lost so much weight! Berthe, not fully understanding what they were saying, kept quiet and continued mechanically performing the automatic gestures that her work required.

While walking along a path bordered by tall gates, she was amazed that all the animals she saw seemed so gentle and serene. But wouldn't they, too, abruptly transform into monsters? She became afraid and started to run, frightened, through the deserted park. Out of breath, she stopped and, letting her gaze wander all around her, had the feeling that she'd been in this place before. But a long time ago, months . . . but a very long time ago; years perhaps . . . Her heart clouded with emotion. The farther into the park she advanced, the more intense her disturbance became; she was stressed, anxious. She passed in front of the elephant, the lion, the panther; she stopped in front of the stag and the doe. THE FOX AND THE RAVEN—THE OAK ONE DAY SAYS TO THE REED . . . At a school desk, Berthe, very young: The oak one day says to the reed, You have reason to complain . . . The burial of her mother. The violence of her father and her own fear. An immense sadness invaded her heart.

Suddenly, there before her, coiled onto itself: the boa. Like thunder after lightning, the shock was abrupt and violent. Blistering, the light that switched on in her. She had just one word, just one name, just one cry: PIERRE!

Then memories formed and unformed, intensified and developed, enough to burn your soul and bruise your heart. She saw every moment spent with Pierre. Every moment. His voice, his smile, his tenderness, his joy, his love, nothing was missing from Berthe's memory. She remained in her room, sprawled on her bed, still as a corpse. Fits of sobbing took hold of her, sometimes lasting hours. In her head everything blurred; she could no longer differentiate days from nights, memories from nightmares. In her hallucinations she saw grotesque beings dancing in pairs and trios in the middle of her bedroom, or sometimes objects that, taking on the face of a man, started to speak. One night a snake appeared to her. Its body extended upright, it shrunk, slowly, until it reached the height of another body, of a man, it seemed to Berthe, whose face, hidden in darkness, she couldn't distinguish. Suddenly it emerged from the darkness to reveal itself to Berthe and she recognized Pierre. He looked at her and smiled sadly. Then, as though to invite her to join them, Pierre gestured to Berthe, but immediately the body of the snake and that of Pierre dissolved into one alone: that of the boa. The snake stared at her with its little beady eyes and Berthe heard it whisper, "It's me, Pierre, come, I'm waiting for you." Then the vision vanished.

The next day Berthe returned to the zoo. She stayed there until closing, in front of the boa, contemplating Pierre.

She went back every day and sat on the little folding chair that she made sure to bring with her. Gazing lovingly at the reptile, she carried on an endless conversation with Pierre.

It was during one of these conversations that Berthe noticed a man next to her, speaking to her: she recognized him as the prison caretaker. Although it was impossible to understand what he was saying, Berthe sensed that this man had bad intentions; he twisted his mouth as he spoke, his eyes were red with rage, and he gesticulated wildly; but the worst was when he lifted his arm, as if to strike her, so she hid her face in her hands. When she lifted her head again, the man had disappeared.

Now, when she saw him at the end of the path coming toward her, she would immediately abandon her folding chair and rush to hide. However, sometimes, too absorbed in her conversation with Pierre, she forgot to watch out for the man's approach, and she didn't see him until he was just a few yards from her, advancing noiselessly like a wolf toward its prey. Apart from the fright the caretaker gave her, Berthe lived in the enchantment of those days that she spent alongside Pierre.

She felt a hand come down brusquely on her shoulder. He was there. She hadn't heard him arrive. He was standing there next to her, taller, larger than normal. He started to speak softly, then more and more loudly. The words cold, mad, sick, deranged recurred often in his mouth. With his chin, with his arm he pointed Berthe in a certain direction. Terrified, she looked at this man with the purple face who was now shaking her by the shoulders. Suddenly understanding that they wanted to separate her from Pierre, that once again they wanted to separate the two of them, she yelled the name Pierre at the boa as though crying for help. With a shrug of the shoulders, the caretaker turned back around.

Spurred by the sudden desire to see her own reflection, she took a small mirror out of her bag and looked at herself in it. The face she saw then, of an unfamiliar woman staring back at her with a smile, overwhelmed her. At the sight of this gaze fixed on her, dark as a forest and severe, Berthe had the strange sensation that the woman wanted to speak to her; that they both had something to say to each other. Suddenly a whistle rang out, then several more, announcing the closing of the zoo. Hurriedly Berthe stood up; she went down the path then ran across the lawn and hid behind a large tree. As in a game of hide and seek when you're afraid of being found, her heart was racing as she waited for the caretaker to pass.

When he arrived, she held her breath as he came to a stop and stared at the empty folding chair, then looked around suspiciously; it was so funny that she nearly burst out laughing. As if he didn't know what to do, he stayed for several minutes next to the folding chair, scratching his chin and glancing warily around him. Then he carried on his way, as though regretfully. This time, Berthe did burst out laughing.

A thought flashed through her mind that incited an immense, indescribable happiness and even dissipated her fear of that man. She felt a supreme calm through all her being, the promise of infinite bliss; she felt, yes, truly: happiness. Emerging from her hiding place, she went down the path, up to the small gate she knew so well, pushed it, and entered.

In the morning the caretaker nearly died of shock at the sight of a woman's body intertwined with that of the boa.

Barbara Wolinard

THE BED

Their presence irks me, and if I could leave I would. Even if I had to crawl I would. But I have to stay here, sitting in my chair, motionless, useless. What business do these gentlemen have milling about my bed? Running around like headless chickens? Will they never leave me in peace? Must they poison even my final days with their presence? Seen from the outside, it's incredible how small my bed is. It's true that when I was in it, my feet and calves hung over the edge with only my torso and thighs able to extend. I had said to them, "I can't possibly spend my whole life in this position." To which they had responded, "No no, you'll see, you'll be like everyone else; in the end you won't even notice it anymore." I envied their optimism. But my life was a nightmare—at least the majority of my life, if I don't count the few months during which I experienced a semblance of happiness thanks to my imagination. Wanting to know exactly how many fingers and toes I had, I started to count the digits on my hands and then those on my feet and then added them all together; since I never reached the same total, I kept having to start over, until the day when I came up with the same number three times in a row, which marked the end of that period that had allowed me both to amuse myself and to stop thinking. I sunk once more into the misery of my life. On the walls of the room I'm in, there are a considerable number of holes, each the size of an eye. At first, since the room had no windows, I thought it might be a ventilation system, but then I noticed that the holes appeared in pairs, and that the distance between them was the same as the distance between two eyes. I realized that from behind the walls of my bedroom, those men were spying on me.

They remove the box spring and mattress from my bed and replace them with a plank of white wood. I wonder why they're doing this. I'd also like to know why they made me get out of bed today. Did they have a feeling something was going to happen to me? Something that would mean they could no longer leave me in my bed and so, instead of waiting for the event to occur, they chose to get out ahead of it? I don't much like these three gentlemen. I don't know what about them arouses my suspicion. The way they all burst into laughter, laughing until they choke, as though someone had said something funny when not a single word has been uttered; it makes me uneasy. After measuring my bed, they transfer it onto four planks, each about fifty centimeters high, and start to saw them. Witnessing the delirious joy and the quasi-demented frenzy with which they saw, I'm beginning to think that these gentlemen live only for work and that without it, they would have no reason TO BE. I fear that my life will have no other meaning than to give them the possibility to exist. Their activity is feverish. I can tell they're anxious to put me there, where I will soon be. I speak about this place and this location only in vague terms because uttering certain words, even in a whisper, can have bad repercussions: it can drive you mad with horror.

So I should change topics. My work could have been a happy digression: sewing. "Sew," they said, "sew," they repeated endlessly, "that will take your mind off of things." All right! But sewing in the dark is terrible. Sometimes the thread forms knots and when you try to undo them, you lose the thread, and then you don't know where it is anymore and you're worried about making sure you start back up in the right place. No one is there to tell you and you can spend months, years, a lifetime groping in the shadows. That's what I did. When, weary, I gave up, they yelled at me, "Pathetic! You think you'll find it if you don't look?" Their bad faith horrified me.

They've finished sawing the planks, and now they're positioning them around my bed frame and nailing them together. The box-like appearance of my new bed provokes a particular anxiety. But I'm wrong to be frightened. Surely they don't plan to put me in that coffin, where I would have to fold myself in two with my legs over my head! If that were the case, I'd have to think these gentlemen, who are clearly insane—it's proof enough that they've sequestered me here in the darkness under the pretext that I have to earn the right to see—might also be downright mean. You can't think that . . . definitely not, because then . . . I've developed a habit of thinking too much and this is where it leads me: a nameless terror, outrageous ideas, distress that fills my heart with tears. A cold sweat drips down my face and my teeth chatter as though I have a fever. I'd like to tell these gentlemen, "Leave, I beg of you. I'm fine here in my

chair, and I ask nothing more of you than to leave me here."
But I can't utter a word, and they're here, gesticulating and
grimacing, buzzing around my bed-box with staggering
expressions of triumph and ferocity in their eyes, all fixed
on me. They've sawed off three of the legs of what was my
bed and now they're hacking away at the fourth. Once
that's gone, the box will rest on the ground.

I'm shivering and trembling nonstop. My head,
suddenly extremely heavy, droops on my chest. Hunted,
I'm struggling to climb out of a well where their flat, rough
hands push me down little by little. After haunting my solitude and throwing a twilit veil over my life, will the shadow
of these three gentlemen pursue me until the end of time?
Eyes shut, I see their pale mouths and their menacing
gazes; ears muffled, I hear their metallic laughter resounding and reverberating endlessly through space. Nothing
around me is palpable anymore; even my body seems to
have abandoned me. My brain spreads before me like an
immense labyrinth; a frightened thought rushes in every
direction, evading me. I go insane trying not to lose it; I
hunt it through the shadows. I have to catch it. It belongs to
me. It has to come back. But it runs off into the night, oblivious to me. In its pursuit I hurtle down bottomless
precipices; I sink into gooey deserts, populated by formless
forms that dash through the pallid night, sometimes emit-
ting strange cries. The thought, as though taunting me,
stops from time to time seemingly to wait for me. My hope
of reaching it in those moments spurs me to overcome
whatever obstacles lie between us at any cost. But just as
quickly, it takes off again with dizzying speed for an obscure
point where I can't find it anymore. I wander looking for it

in the opacity of the night for centuries on end. Hope turns to despair and reason crumbles.

The three gentlemen suddenly appear in front of me; with an impenetrable gaze they scrutinize me and then murmur, "He's searching for it. Now he's ours," and they disappear while I continue to make my way through the shadows. "Where are you?" I cry, suddenly frightened at no longer being able to see the thought and, because I let myself be distracted by these gentlemen, not knowing which way it went. "I'm here," it responds in a small, distant voice. "Come, I'm waiting for you." A mocking laugh accompanies these words. I rush blindly into the night; passing glacial shadows, I run without stopping, prey to panic. Sometimes I see the three gentlemen. Their sharp gazes follow me as I continue to make my way through the night. They're buried under thousands of boxes. One of the boxes bursts into flames as I pass. I think that one's mine.

Barbara Rodimard

TAXI

Head heavy. Full of fog. Must have fallen asleep. Don't remember getting in a taxi. When? Where? Heading for what destination? Impossible to remember. Could ask the driver. Around the man's bald head, like a ribbon, a large iron band. The band so tight that the flesh bulges around it. Why that iron ribbon? Fear. For a long time I couldn't go out. Complete disorientation. Shapes of houses, immense rectangular blocks of steel. No roof. Others sometimes pyramid-shaped. Dizzying. Cars, monstrous beasts moving in every direction. No one outside really. Through the open front windows the wind blows to the back and freezes me. Near the houses, bizarre machines fly over the city. The man's neck, rigid and dry. Search for face in rearview; meet only gaze of the man, cold, glacial, inhuman, staring at me. Squish down so as not to be seen. Afraid, but say nothing. Am sure it's for the best. Strange, this emptiness in my head, like waking up after an operation. Have had many operations I think. Anxiety. Sweat dripping into my eyes. Trembling all through my body. Iron band around his bald head, bulge of flesh all around. Neck rigid and dry. People on the boulevard. Just the time to see a few, their legs, arms, and torsos are made of metal. Only human heads. Eye staring at me in rearview. Say nothing. Would surely have grave consequences. Sense it.

Before: trees, flowers. Now: iron, stone. No birds. No cries of children. World of silence. Panic. All alone. Where are my friends. Surely had friends before. Everyone lets us pass. Steel traffic man too. Makes you think. Very important not to think. Long line of cars stalled on the road. Brusque jerk of the steering wheel; accelerator. Rush straight ahead and crash. Continue on our way as though nothing happened. In rearview, glacial and scrutinizing eye fixed on me. Keep it together. Vital. Try to smile, manage only a grimace. Fear. Tragic streets. Iron atmosphere. Weakness. Empty head. Keep it together. Neck rigid and dry. Iron band. Bald head. Speak to this man. Necessary. Personal conviction that it's necessary. So:

"Where are we going, monsieur?"

"Nowhere in particular. We're taking a drive."

Gaze in rearview watching me. Don't react. Act natural. His voice:

"Are you happy? Do you like it?"

"What?"

"Everything you see: the people, the town, the houses?"

Sense a trick question. Respond in the right way.

"Yes, good. All very good. Very pleasant."

Eye staring at me.

"Really, are you not even a little bit surprised?"

Heart starts to thump. Panic. Personal conviction that I have already heard these questions several times. The same ones (or almost). In identical circumstances (or almost). But a long time ago surely. Always resulted in anni-hilation, sleep, vertigo, waking, nausea, distress.

Respond in the right way. What's the right way? Venture:

"Am never surprised, monsieur, and never will be."

Eye scrutinizing me.

"You're doing much better."

"I was sick?"

"Not exactly, but in a way, yes."

Vast shiver. Terror. To jump turn handle of door. Locked. Am trapped inside. Keep it together. Vital. Big black dog beautiful shining coat crosses. Accelerator. Ram straight into the animal. Shock. Scream. Groans. Moans. Turn around. Dog in pool of blood, immobile, maybe dead. Horror. The man laughs loudly. Don't scream but:

"Why, monsieur?"

"Because it's not important."

Rearview gaze fixed on me. Frozen with fear. Just say nothing. Bald head, iron-band-neck-rigid-and-dry. Abrupt memory. Immense room; bare white walls. Where? When? How long? Site of unspeakable distress where heart and soul are suspended. Echoes of voices: "Operation tomor-row seven o'clock. Operation tomorrow nine o'clock. Operation tonight seven o'clock. Operation tonight midnight . . . operation . . . operation . . ." Groans from all around, plaintive sighs. Where? When? Eye in rearview riveted to me. Don't be seen. Check out car. Hide. Jump. No obstacle but brusque jerk of steering wheel. On sidewalk three people, human, not made of steel, stand waiting.

Gaunt gaunt faces; immense eyes. Drive onto sidewalk. Frightened recoil of three people. Accelerator. Brief pursuit. Mow down all three. I scream. Everything spins.

Eyelids heavy. Impossible to open my eyes. Sprawled. Probably in bed. Odor of ether. Want to leave, flee. Immobility. Near me, very near, two voices:

"When did it happen?"

"During the rehabilitation walk. She screamed and then she fainted."

"At what point?"

"At the sidewalk."

"At the sidewalk! So soon! She's a lost cause then, incurable. Write down: one injection tonight for bed 4327."

Barbara M.

THE SPONGE

Before it's too late, I want them to know the truth: no matter what these people think, I am not guilty of the crimes they've accused me of since I was born. I don't know why they decided, once and for all, to be against me. Which wouldn't have been so terrible if I hadn't been subjected to their slander, their aggression, their surly gazes, and their sardonic smiles throughout my whole life, even from those closest to me: my wife, to be precise. How many times did I catch her staring at me, hiding behind the bathroom windows, while I was messing around and making faces at myself in the mirror, or spying on me from the doorway as I yanked the dog's tail. If I wanted to, I could cite numerous examples that would prove just how hellish my life is.

Lately objects, too, have started to behave like these people: they've turned against me. A knife I was using to scrape the dog's skin after pulling out its hair suddenly cut into my thumb; a pine needle sneakily stabbed me as I was walking naked through the garden; a shutter pinched my finger. Now, out of fear of these objects, I no longer dare move and spend entire days sitting in my armchair in the middle of the room. When my wife comes (I have however forbidden her from entering that room while I'm there), she looks at me inquisitively. But I pretend not to notice until the moment when brusquely I get up and, standing right in front of her, thumb my nose at her. Her frightened face makes me contort with laughter, as does her voice when she murmurs with a feigned tenderness: "Pierre, sweetie, you know I mean you no harm." "Sweetie." Those humiliations they inflict on me, day after day, are becoming unbearable.

Especially that sponge that's been lying in wait for me for three days now (I formally forbade anyone from moving it). This sponge and I, we have a score to settle.

I tiptoe into the kitchen. As expected, the sponge is there, enormous (much too large for a sponge) and round, very round. Too round for me not to see immediately that this sponge is the Earth itself. I decide on the spot to eradicate the sad planet. But I have to be careful: I have to do it in such a way that the sponge doesn't suspect anything. Noiselessly I advance toward the chair and, sitting down, place my two arms horizontally on the table to form a wall. Then, extremely slowly, I let my arms creep in its direction. My muscles knot beneath the skin. But I hold firm and advance undetected, centimeter by centimeter, toward the insolent ball.

The sun begins to set. The nervous tension created by this slow movement is exhausting. My body drenched with sweat, panting, I continue to inch my arms toward it; soon they graze it. Nausea and a strong desire to vomit run through me. I start to push the earthly globe slowly, slowly, to bring it to that ultimate point, with no way out, when it will have no option but to roll into the abyss. The idea of destroying it makes me dizzy, floods me with an unspeakable happiness. I grit my teeth so as not to let my joy erupt.

The kitchen has expanded. I can't see the walls anymore. The space around me is immense, infinite, and at the center of that space is the Earth on the table, which now offers a strange resistance to my arms shattered with fatigue; they go flat, are soon no more than half of their original thickness. Toward the middle of the night my arms are meager, useless sticks. Tears of rage flood my eyes. My throat is gripped with sobs. Like a statue, my wife stands immobile near me. Her face is ice. I rush at her and punch her in the jaw. Without a word, but with a deafening sound, she falls to the tile. I sit back down and suddenly see the ball turning, slowly at first, then at a dizzying speed. Flames soar from all sides. Drunk with joy at watching it burn, I want to grasp it between my hands to break it, but it escapes me and as it twirls, it leads me in its wake. My heart bursts. I crumble to the ground.

I open my eyes. What happened? Why am I in this dark cell, lying on a pallet? A key enters the lock. The door creaks open. A man says to me, "Come. Today is your sentencing." I follow him through many corridors and enter a room full of people. Someone says that I killed my wife. A man on the stand says that even as a child I was mean. A fat woman—my wet nurse, apparently—confirms that even as a baby, a perverse instinct incited me to bite her as she was breastfeeding me. Other people cycle through, burdening me with their dismal, sad expressions, as though regretfully. But implacably. My father and my mother are also present (at least I'm told it's them; I've seen them so few times, practically never), but I don't recognize them. They explain that they were forced to put me in a reform school very early on because even as a child I had evil tendencies, and then they sent me to a juvenile detention center. The crowd pities them, shakes their heads, and shoots hateful looks in my direction.

I think to myself that it's a real shame I didn't manage to topple the Earth while I was in the kitchen. From here, I believe it will be impossible.

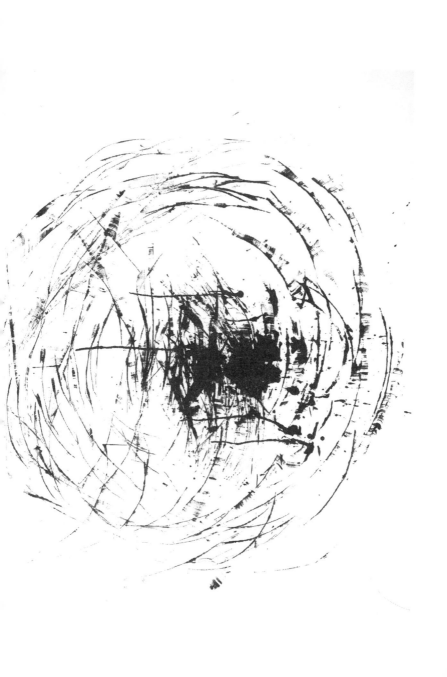

HAPPINESS

Clarisse de Karadec, née Desanges, hurried to the table; the deed to her house was there, where she'd put it the night before, amid the various papers and the enormous heap of envelopes. God, she'd been scared! Joyously she embraced the precious document and set it back down on the table. As she glanced mechanically at the envelopes spilling in every direction that all bore her name written in the same tall, dancing handwriting, she noticed with a smile that they hadn't been opened. But when she saw that many didn't have a stamp anymore, imagining that one of her friends must be a collector and was nabbing them while she slept, she couldn't help but laugh.

Waking up in her house for the first time, she was delighted to already feel at home there: "MY HOUSE!" she shouted in a radiant voice, glancing around the room for maybe the hundredth time since the day before. "Ravishing," she murmured, leaning against the wall in order to fully take in the room, "truly ravishing, a bit bare perhaps; I'll need to buy statues, heaps of statues." She remembered seeing some recently that were very beautiful . . . in a park . . . or in a forest. "Life is wonderful." If she hadn't resolved to act with the utmost discretion toward the friends she'd invited to spend a few days in her house, she would gladly have gone to say a quick hello. *How astonishing life is, how surprising, wonderful, and unpredictable*, she thought. Who would ever have thought, even a few weeks ago, that today she would be in HER HOUSE! And the sound of the sea that would never leave her, such rapture! She ran to the window, opened it wide, and inhaled the fresh air with delight. That sea she saw stretch before her infinitely, as far as the eye could see, fascinated her. She promised herself that as soon as it was nice out, she would bathe in the sea and bathe in the sun too; her body needed it so badly! In the meantime, she would exercise every morning. She was very proud of still being able to jump like a little girl even though she was more than thirty years old, and she could also climb up a rope like a squirrel on a tree. She gasped; fully dressed people were entering the water. Eyes gazing into the distance, she saw streets, cars, haggard people walking on their own and seemingly oblivious to others. She held on to the window frame to steady herself; they advanced slowly into the open water and then, suddenly, they disappeared. Softly she fell to the ground.

When she came to, it seemed the sun had set. *The weather is turning gray*, she thought sadly. *I need to light a candle, that'll brighten things up.* Comforted by the idea, she got up, slowly crossed the room, and lay down on her bed. If the telephone had been connected, she would have immediately called one of her friends, anyone at all, just for the pleasure of hearing a voice. *Luckily there are birds . . . the sea and the birds, so I'm never alone . . .* She stretched voluptuously, a smile on her lips. Suddenly she thought of what she would have for lunch: caviar, bread, champagne;

she jumped up. When she put on her gloves, coat, and hat and looked at herself in the mirror, she was astonished that the woman she saw staring back was her: Clarisse de Karadec. If not for the color of her clothes, she wouldn't have recognized herself; she was pleased that for some time now, or even longer than that perhaps, she didn't remember exactly, she never bought clothes unless they were black, mauve, or white. It's not that she particularly liked those colors, but that's what she had decided one day, she didn't know why anymore, and when she tried to remember she couldn't, but became infinitely sad.

In the street there weren't many people; the rare few were walking quickly through the rain. Clarisse thought they seemed tense, unhappy; that always struck her, out in the street, those faces full of desolation and sadness as though they weren't, like her, happy to be alive. A bakery full of light and cakes wrested her from her thoughts; she paused for a moment to look in the window and entered the shop. Standing, she gulped down three éclairs, a rum baba, and two tarts. Then she paid and left.

A formation of planes passing over the city made her jump; lifting her head she watched them set off fireworks; it was splendid! She had never before seen anything so beautiful. Alone on the sidewalk—the passersby had taken shelter behind carriage doors—Clarisse, dazzled, admired the shapes in the sky. Then abruptly it all stopped and the sky went dark again. The street seemed sad: Always the same stores! the same narrow sidewalks! the same street lights! Always everywhere the same thing! But elsewhere there wasn't the noise of the sea audible in the distance. Over there was missing that air full of salt and marine fragrance that for her was like a light perfume, a promise of happiness. She was eager now to get back home, to HER house, to be in her beautiful room, but first she had to buy the champagne . . . the caviar . . . To save time she started to run. At the end of the street she took another street to an intersection; crossing it she reached the store at the corner and entered. It was packed. Waiting for her turn to be served, she examined the vegetables: they were splendid! Tomatoes fat like pumpkins with a skin so fine and soft that it reminded her of baby skin. It must be wonderful to bite into them, but she hated tomatoes. *Too bad!* she thought. *These must be quite good . . .* A pat of butter started to melt before her eyes, spreading over the counter and proving that it must not have been as cold as people were saying. They said it was 33 or 34 degrees—madness! And yet everyone seemed to believe it because they were all dressed in warm clothes! Fortunately she had stopped being surprised by anything some time ago! The butter was now a large waterfall; concerned about the puddle forming on the ground behind the shelves, she bent down. "Can I help you, madame?" Clarisse jolted back up. The saleswoman, a smile on her lips, was standing next to her. As she was being served, Clarisse de Karadec was moved by how friendly the saleswoman was to her, and the owner at the register too, who, when their gazes met, flashed her big gracious smiles. To repay their kindness she decided she would always buy her groceries in this store. Without worrying about the passersby she jostled on her way and who furiously grumbled through their teeth or called her an old lunatic, she finally arrived in front of her house and felt an immense happiness upon seeing it again. "Life is marvelous," she murmured, climbing the stairs wearily, "and everyone is so nice . . ." On the second-floor landing she saw two of her friends; she would have liked to stop and say hello to them, but she didn't want them to feel obliged to invite her to lunch or dinner, and so she simply nodded her head at them. They responded with a friendly smile and went on their way; her friends' discreet courtesy touched her and she was glad to have invited them.

Back in her room she saw the wide-open window and the soaked ground. *I'm incorrigible*, she thought, laughing and leaning over the hand rail to gaze at the sea; but she saw nothing; only the smashing sound of the waves resounding in her head proved that the ocean was still there. There was a thick fog before her, then, suddenly the sea, howling, unleashed, hollowed with grooves, bloated with waves furiously furling and unfurling. Fascinated by the deafening sight, Clarisse de Karadec kept her eyes riveted to the ocean. Body tense and heart alert, with neither a gesture nor a blink she participated in that raging, thunderous unleashing of the sea: "Men might be drowning . . . Men have drowned," she murmured. "One day a man drowned . . . One day a man drowned," she repeated, with the vague feeling that through these words she would remember; that she HAD TO remember. An immense sadness invaded her heart, and for an instant she was aware that her brain was an abyss into which her thoughts were sinking irremediably. She was suddenly very cold; she left the window and on the other side of the room she lit the small gas radiator that served as her heater.

Now sitting in a chair with a radio on her knees, she listened gaily to a song; nothing subsisted of the tidal wave that had just so deeply unsettled her. With a stunned glance around her room, she declared that she would buy statues, statues that would nearly reach the ceiling . . . she had seen one that day in a park . . . she would just find that one . . . and then she would throw a costume ball . . . all the men would be naval officers. Radiant, she stood up and started to dance. Abruptly realizing that she was dying of hunger, Clarisse de Karadec pulled out the provisions she'd bought and put together a plate with two slices of ham, a petit suisse, and an egg, then grabbed the bottle of cider and poured herself a large glass. God, it was good! She had no idea she was so thirsty! She poured herself another glass, placed it on the table without drinking it, and sunk her teeth into the ham, which was simply exquisite; she was about to serve herself the last slice when she was seized by a brusque fit of laughter thinking again of the caviar and the champagne. It was so funny, their habit of always giving her the wrong thing! She couldn't get a hold of herself, tears were streaming down her face, she hiccuped . . . Once she'd calmed down, she felt a sudden fatigue. With her head hunched over her chest, she remained drooped in the chair with her eyes closed, listening to the gentle rustling of the sea.

Although she had barely slept, when Clarisse woke up and saw that it was nice out, she jumped out of bed and ran to the window. In the blue of the sky, which she deemed as blue as the blue of her eyes, a golden ball hovered immobile in space. She was marveling at the splendor of that globe when suddenly she noticed that nothing was suspending it and that it could fall at any moment; seized with fright she shut her eyes. But suddenly realizing that she'd be able to swim, her fear vanished on the spot. She ran to the armoire, took out a cardboard box, and opened it. There was her bathing suit, wrapped in tissue paper, mauve with a white trim, it was quite pretty; she was not disappointed. She had bought it a few days earlier in Paris, although she hadn't known at the time that she would be living by the sea. Maybe if I hadn't bought it, I wouldn't have come to live here, who knows? She burst out laughing. When she had put it on and looked at herself in the mirror, Clarisse couldn't believe her eyes: could it be possible that she was this beautiful? It was inconceivable. Head on, from the side, from an angle, from behind—she was perfect! An envelope under her door that she glimpsed in the mirror wrested her from her contemplation. Her heart racing, she bent down for the letter. Maybe it was the letter she'd been waiting for? The tall, dancing handwriting reassured her. But why had she written DESANGES instead of KARADEC! This error, for which she could only blame herself, left her perplexed for a moment.

It wasn't a big deal, the important thing was to have the letter. A smile spread across her lips.

I'll open it with the others, later, when I'm old, she thought gaily, throwing the letter on the table with the rest.

She was about to go out for a swim when she had the thought that it would be much simpler, and also much more agreeable, to dive directly from her window. As she admired the ocean before her eyes, gray and gleaming like asphalt, Clarisse enjoyed imagining the pleasure she would feel soon, in just a moment, as her body slipped between the waves. But was that the only thing she desired from the sea, this pleasure, this joy? Wasn't there, down in the depths of the ocean, some hidden treasure that she had lost . . . A strange emotion, a wild, insane, delirious hope took hold of her. "Life is marvelous," Clarisse mumbled. She filled her lungs with air and with a thrust of her whole body, she jumped.

Avenue de l'Opéra, an ambulance picked up the body of a woman in her sixties, crushed on the sidewalk. She was wearing nothing but a mauve bathing suit with a white trim.

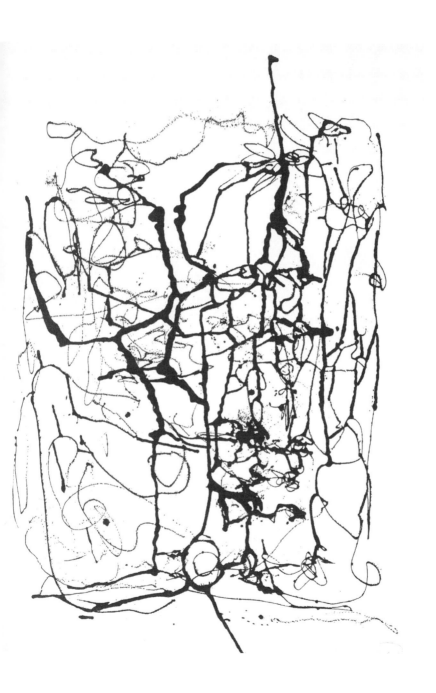

I'M ALONE AND IT'S NIGHT

They came into the bedroom and told me not to move. Maybe that's why two people—nurses, I think—strapped my body to the bed so that the bed and I became one and the same. Since they left my arms free, I stick them in the air from time to time. I find it amusing. But normally I keep them still, splayed on the sheet. They give me injections. Many injections. They take forever and go deep. But apparently they're necessary. Some man or other enters my room. Generally he begins by watching me, observing me for a very long time without saying a word. Then he orders me to open my mouth and close my eyes (I obey this order less and less willingly), and he puts a needle in my mouth that pierces my cheek from the inside through to the outside. Despite the pain, I don't scream, because apparently they don't like that. That's what they told me the first time. And that was it, they never said anything to me again: they sang, the first man a military march and the second a hymn. Then they started to leave the needle in my mouth for hours on end. Even days. But not often, because I get too agitated. They want me patient and docile.

To be the object of so much attention worries me sometimes since, in the end, I've never asked them for anything, not for a single favor, despite what one might be tempted to believe. No, it's because of their own boss that they act this way, as part of a plan unknown to me. At least so it seems. Sometimes, I want them all dead. I think they might suspect this, for almost as soon as I start to wish it, one or another of these men immediately appears, stares at me angrily, and threatens me with his fist as I perform my mea culpa and tears of helplessness stream from my eyes. What astonishes me is that they all insist on not saying anything to me, not explaining anything. For example: Why am I here? . . . When did I arrive? . . . Do I have to stay here forever? Did I have a life before this? And if so, where? When I ask these questions, they keep mum. Why, I wonder . . . I must have lost my memory. Unless I never had one, which amounts to the same thing. Often, at night, someone I can't see stealthily enters my bedroom and holds a lamp up to my face, turning it on and off over and over for an indeterminate amount of time, as if he were expecting something from this little game. Nothing ever happens except inside of me: a sense of panic that grows more intense each time. There are in fact many other worrying things about this place. I would prefer not to talk about them. At least not right now.

I would rather, for example, talk about my room. If it were beautiful. But it's black, sordid, filthy; its walls are dirtied with dreadful stains teeming with bands of worms and a multitude of beasts, black and engorged with my blood. This room is a bedroom in name only. It would be more accurate to call it a hovel, a cupboard, or a closet. But that would be too embarrassing for me. Yesterday, they promised they'd feed me today. I've been waiting ever since. It's nice that they care for me. I mean: that they feed me. They give me everything here. That's why (if I really think about it) I would be wrong to complain. What depresses me the most is not having a single moment of solitude. There's a continuous coming and going through my bedroom. People mill about and cram in to such an extent that sometimes there's not enough air for me to breathe. They are shapeless beings, often missing a limb or two, sometimes their head. But they don't seem unhappy. Nor happy either for that matter. When they're not around and I can finally be alone, there's an eye on the ceiling surveilling me. Sometimes, when I can no longer stand the sight of it, I spit into the air at it, but it's no use: the spit falls back onto my bed. Just now, I still had the needle in my mouth when a hairy, cheerful woman entered pushing a rolling table with a tray and food. I went wild at the thought of eating. But since they hadn't taken the needle out of my mouth, the woman came back later and removed the tray. They really lack organization in this house. If they wanted me to eat, you'd think they'd let me do so. I'd like to know what compels them to act this way. Not long after, they came to take the needle out. The surge of blood I vomited soiled the entire sheet. This position—sprawled on my back and unable to move—grows more and more painful for me. They should be able to see that. I almost wonder if they're doing it on purpose, if it's not some kind of game. I can't think of what happened last night without a heavy heart. A man, colossally tall and large, entered my bedroom with another man who was very small. When the first, addressing the second, asked how I was doing, I heard him answer, "He's making progress, Master." The "Master" responded

with an abrupt and inextinguishable burst of laughter
which nevertheless filled me with a wild hope. I thought to
myself that, if this was the Master (I had only seen his
subordinates up to that point), he might clarify some things
that were important to me. All I had to do was question him
at the opportune moment and even, if need be, beg for
mercy—for he seemed like a good man—and then I would
finally learn the truth and my fate would improve. Arro-
gantly, he ordered the small man to see himself out. As
soon as he had done so, the Master went to the far end of
the bedroom and, hunching slightly, glued his eye to a hole
in the wall that I hadn't noticed before. While the man
watched without moving, my curiosity was so intense that
I felt a tingling sensation all over my body. What he saw
seemed to please him, for I heard him chuckle. Sometimes,
turning toward me, he would give me a complicit wink, as
though to reassure me that I had nothing to worry about,
that everything was going very well, going how he wanted
in any event. When he came back over to me, he examined
me for a long time with an expression of amusement, all
while rubbing his hands together with obvious pleasure. It
seemed like a good moment to speak to him; I opened my
mouth, but the inside of it was in such a pitiful state, full of
wounds and pus, and my flesh so swollen that it was impossible for me to say a word. He leaned over me, flicked my
nose, ears, and chin and pronounced in conclusion, "Good
. . . very good . . . perfect . . . absolutely perfect." Although
gentle and melodious, his voice didn't comfort me, maybe
because I was wondering how the moribund sight of me,
bound to a wretched pallet, could possibly satisfy him.
Before leaving the room, he returned to the wall, glanced
quickly through the hole, and took off running. I screamed

so much when they cut off my arms (they cut them off yesterday) that I'm still completely debilitated from it. It must have aggravated them to hear my screams because they gagged me toward the end. As I was writhing around, they said to me, "Stop moving so much all the time. Later, you'll see, you'll be a new man and you'll be able to leave the house." I admit that this last phrase eased my suffering and soon I remained perfectly still. So I was going to leave this place! Maybe they cut off my arms because there's no need for arms "over there." Otherwise, why would they have done it? They have no reason to be malicious. For some time now, instead of putting a needle in my mouth, they've started injecting my eyes and following it up with some drops. What's strange is that ever since, I've struggled to see; if they keep at it, I'm certain I'll go completely blind. It's impossible to guess the end goal of these operations I'm subjected to. But I wish I knew; it would be a great comfort. Maybe it would free my mind from the gnawing anxiety that seizes and torments me relentlessly. I was so afraid yesterday when I saw them arrive with the stretcher and the Master loaded my body onto it; I worried they were going to bring me to the room with all the tools and cut off my legs. They didn't do that; only my nose and ears. They also tampered with my eyes and now I can't see anything at all. The man wearing a mask said to me before he began, "Now I'm going to need you to give me a hand." I wondered if that was really necessary, but they didn't ask my permission, otherwise I would have refused. I've noticed it isn't really their style to ask my opinion. I don't speak about the moral and physical suffering I endure. Atrocious suffering. What good would it do me? And I'm not the only one, as evidenced by these people who mill about my bedroom. If only we could have spoken to each other . . . exchanged ideas about this or that, maybe it could have benefited us in some way. But it must have been as impossible for them as it was for me, otherwise they would have done so. I recognized from his voice that the Master had just entered my bedroom. He told them to remove the bandages from my head. Someone obeyed him, sitting on my bed to unroll the strip. When he reached the final loop, rather than peeling it gently from the wounds on my nose and ears, he ripped it off with an incomprehensible violence. I would certainly never do things the way they do. Then I felt them remove the sheets from the bed.

The Master must have leaned down very close to me, for I heard him whisper, "We've done everything we can for you. I've stacked all the odds in your favor. Now it's up to you to take advantage! You may leave. You will stand up and I will accompany you to the exit."

Frightened by these words for, given my state, I found the moment poorly timed to send me off, I showed my displeasure by pounding my two feet against the wall. They calmed me down by pouring a bucket of boiling water over my face and my entire body. As I attempted to stand up, I wobbled on my legs and fell heavily to the ground. They led me haphazardly down numerous hallways. If I'd still had arms, I would surely have wrapped them around their legs. Then I arrived at a place that must have been the exit, for I heard the Master ask them to open the door. Immediately a glacial wind walloped my naked body.

"Go!" said the Master, pushing me out with a tranquil insistence, "*you are a free man.*"

Now, I'm alone and it's night.

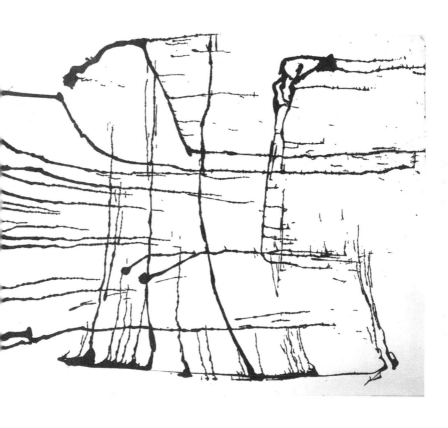

THE VAULT

Transcribed by Marguerite Duras

MARGUERITE DURAS: **If you had managed to write "The Vault," would that story have been the only one in the collection about a real-life event?**
BARBARA MOLINARD: Yes, the only one.

You've agreed to tell me what happened to you?
Yes. We can try it this way.

One day, I'm in the sixteenth arrondissement. I'm walking along a very high wall. I don't know what's behind it, then suddenly I see that it's a cemetery. I enter. Now I enjoy strolling through cemeteries, but at the time, not at all. I enter and I begin to walk. Then I arrive in front of a temple of love. There's a gate around it. I push on the gate: it opens. There's a staircase in the center of the temple. I go down. There are twenty stairs. On my way down, I feel a sense of calm. When I reach the bottom I'm struck by the silence. The room is a half circle. I see four tombs in the back. The silence that reigns there is unlike any other; it's as though I've gone deaf. As I linger there, sitting on the stairs, an immense calm slowly invades me. Several times

I think to myself that I should go back up. (My husband must be waiting for me.) But I stay there, tranquil and happy. ACCEPTED.

Can you talk about this sense of calm?
In the moment I wouldn't have known how to describe it. Now I think it was because I was outside, outside of people, the street, everything. Which is a good place to be, really. There had always been a gap, an obstacle between them or the world and me. There, I was separated. When I went back to the bistro, I saw them laughing, talking, drinking, as if nothing had happened. I fled. I don't remember what happened next.

Did this vault remind you of something?
No. Nothing. At that moment my husband, my children, no longer mattered to me at all. I wasn't thinking. I felt good; that's all I can say.

Happy?
No, not happy. Good.

What happened after your visit to the vault?
I don't know what happened for the next two days. I don't remember at all.

I know that on the third day it was clear: I had to spend three days and three nights in that vault. I told my husband. He was fine with it. He didn't voice any objection. From that moment, I started to plan what I would need to live in that vault. I made a list so I wouldn't forget anything:

candles, two or three bottles of Badoit, a bottle of red wine, warm clothes, salami, bread, and of course a sleeping bag.

Books?
Yes. That should have been the most important thing, but I realize now that I'd forgotten them. I didn't have a sleeping bag. I called a friend who had lent hers out. The lack of sleeping bag was very concerning.

Did you tell your children the truth?
Yes, I told them the truth, I had nothing to hide. The reaction was violent.

My plan was to wait for the next day to enter the vault—with or without a sleeping bag. The next day was WEDNESDAY. I would enter the vault WEDNESDAY. I would return Saturday morning. I didn't want to spend the weekend there, there would be too many people.

When did you learn that you wouldn't be going to the vault?
Tuesday night. My husband came home. He told me that he'd seen the doctor. The doctor had told him it would be very bad *for him and for the children* if I went to the vault.

Tuesday night I sleep one hour. I wake up exhausted. The physical pains begin that night. I had horrifying muscle aches. It took me an incredible amount of time just to turn over in my bed. From that night on, every night, the pains are different. I have pains in my neck, my back, my limbs. Then, cold sweats. And then, shortness of breath. I couldn't breathe anymore.

During the day the pains passed. They would come back at night and wake me up. I slept very little.

For a month, often I would lose all contact with the person I was speaking to. I saw them. Then, all of a sudden, I no longer heard them: their lips would be moving and I wouldn't hear any sound. It was quite pleasant.

At a certain point the pains are so intense that I agree to see a doctor. I tell him everything. I tell him about the vault and the terrible suffering I'm experiencing. He tells me, "I'm not worried about your suffering. These pains are a blessing. You should expect more, and for them to become even more violent. This suffering HEALS you. You are very lucky."

He sketches a brain and tries to explain to me what could have happened inside my brain if it hadn't been unleashed inside my body instead. He explains that for another month or two I will feel all sorts of physical aches but that they will disappear on their own. Suddenly I lose all contact with him. I see his lips move; I can't hear what he's saying anymore. Then I hear him again.

You didn't understand what he was saying to you?
It intrigued me and worried me. I wasn't afraid in the moment. It was only after the fact that I was afraid of what might have happened. I had already drawn the connection between my aches and the vault. The pains were an extreme version of the pains I would have felt had I slept on the ground, directly on the stone floor.

Later on, I went to Brittany, alone. But my daughters were already there. I wrote to them that I was coming but that I didn't want to see them unless I ran into them by chance. Which is in fact what happened. I had a room like I'd never seen before. It was on the first floor. It was long and narrow. There was just enough space for me to pass between the bed and the armoire. I asked for a table that was as wide as the room. At the back of the room was a window that looked onto an empty lot. I went out very little. I was very happy in that room. It suited me perfectly.

What did you do in that room?
I wrote. I have no idea what.

Did you draw a connection between the room and the vault?
Yes, but not right away, only over the course of the month.

Do you still think of the vault?
Sometimes. The doctor told me that if I had gone into that vault, it would have been very bad for me. In my mind, the pain I experienced was due to the fact that they had DEPRIVED me of the vault.

Do you still think it's normal for someone to want to spend three days in a vault?
Oh yes, completely. The doctor tells me, reasonably, that it's madness. For me, in me, not at all.

Death is in all your stories.
Yes, death, it's the only surprise left, because there are absolutely none in life. So it's attractive to me. I wasn't afraid at all. I believe that after death, something interesting happens. I am not at all religious. In any event, death

must be better than life. We have a chance at seizing—in death—something that, in life, is elusive.

Perhaps you're talking about the moment of death and not death itself?
No. I don't think about the moment of death, that doesn't interest me.

What is the void?
It's this. The void is what we live. It's bullshit. It's in everything, the cities, the people. The human race should be better. We are very mediocre.

You said to me, "MAYBE I NEED TO DRUG MYSELF TO BE AT MY BEST."
Yes. I won't seek to go beyond myself, to be inundated with myself. I would just like to be able to be myself.

TRANSLATOR'S NOTE

It was the summer of 2017 and my apartment didn't have air conditioning, so I spent most of my free time sitting by one body of water or another around Rhode Island. I was doing research on Marguerite Duras's nonfiction writing for a cotranslation project with Olivia Baes that would become *Me & Other Writing*, a collection of Duras's essays. Under the shade of a tree by the lake in Lincoln Woods, I was reading through *Le monde extérieur* when I stumbled upon Duras's preface to Barbara Molinard's *Viens*, an unfamiliar book that immediately piqued my interest. A funny feeling crept over me as I read Duras's description of Molinard's work. I was struck by the lines "What we've collected in this book represents a very small portion—maybe a hundredth—of what Barbara has written over these eight years. The rest was destroyed." There's Molinard's prolificness, a clearly voracious need to write, and then there's the destruction, a sign that the writing wasn't doing what it was supposed to do. Or that it was, but publishing the writing wasn't the point. In either case, this "we" indicated that Duras was close enough to this woman, admired her writing enough, that she felt Molinard's work needed to be saved from her "enemy," Molinard herself, who ripped to pieces everything she wrote almost as soon as it was put down on paper.

Duras's preface is also smattered with entire sentences in capital letters. An aggressive proclamation that "EVERYTHING BARBARA MOLINARD HAS WRITTEN HAS BEEN TORN TO SHREDS." Not Duras's style—Duras taking on Molinard's style, a form of tribute. The words "enemy," "suffering," "agony," "absolute night" jumped out at me. Duras was telling a story, about a woman and her loneliness, her devastation, her hope that somehow writing would ease the pain and allow her to express something "neither invented nor dreamed" but "lived." I was compelled by Duras's insistence that some remnant of this woman's work had to be witnessed and celebrated. The capital letters communicated an urgency, but there was also something disturbing about them. Barbara Molinard was a woman disturbed, and Marguerite Duras was a woman moved by her disturbance. And then there was me, another woman, moved by how moved Duras was by Molinard's disturbance, the two of us moved by one woman's attempt to render an intolerable life slightly more tolerable.

Barbara Molinard (1921–1986) was born in Paris and lived out her days in Auvers-sur-Oise with her husband, the filmmaker and photographer Patrice Molinard, and their two daughters, Agnès and Laurence. She married Patrice in 1945 and worked with him in his studio until 1960, when she began to dedicate herself entirely to writing. Despite all the years of devotion to her craft, despite the countless pages she wrote, *Viens* is the only book that survives. Her mental health struggles, combined, perhaps, with crippling fear or self-doubt, kept her trapped in a destructive cycle that prevented her from ever sending any pages to a publisher. So what happened when Marguerite Duras and Patrice Molinard finally wrested these fourteen stories from Molinard's "enemy" and brought them to Éditions Mercure de France, who published the book in 1969? Seemingly, not much. The book fell out of print, and the rights eventually reverted back to Molinard's two daughters. I don't know how many people have read *Viens*, or the stories excerpted in the journal *La Nouvelle Revue Française* in 1962 under the title "Paniques," which is where the English title I chose comes from. Despite Duras's endorsement, Molinard did not go on to publish anything more. It seems unlikely she could have been persuaded to do so. But what I read that day by the water immediately got under my skin: I had to read this book. Who was Barbara Molinard, and what would her writing sound like, feel like?

I am often asked, as a literary translator, how I find the projects I pitch. The answer is that it's usually instinct, a vague gut feeling I get when I read an excerpt from a book, hear someone talking about a book, see a book on a shelf, find out about an author. I get the sense that the book is going to speak to me in some deep way that nothing I've read in English has, that some dormant part of me will awaken after living inside the book, inhabiting and regurgitating the author's words in my translation. That there is a piece of me I'm not yet fully aware of that exists in these books like some kind of deranged reverse horcrux, and that I am somehow less alive, less myself, before I've absorbed a given text into me. That's the feeling I had when I read the preface to *Viens*. I knew this book would be eerie, unsettling, utterly exacting in its expression of the alienation of womanhood, motherhood, wifehood. The solitude within the family unit. The unbearable within the ordinary. The placidness within the panic and vice versa. The need to write a way out of something that can't otherwise be expressed.

And so I set about trying to find a copy. It wasn't available anywhere online. The French publisher didn't have a PDF. I walked into the Providence Public Library one day, knowing about interlibrary loans but with very little hope in this particular case. I was amazed to find that my local librarian could borrow it from the Princeton University Library and have it to me in two weeks. The day the book arrived, I speed-walked down the hill to the library and arrived out of breath. In my memory I'm in a red dress, but that can't be right. The book was so unassuming with its plain white cover. It seemed like some kind of heist that I was able to walk out the door with it. I took it straight to the bookstore where I worked at the time and began reading it between helping customers.

Barbara Molinard

Viens

MERCURE DE FRANCE

As soon as I read the first story, "The Plane from Santa Rosa," I knew the book was exactly what I'd imagined it would be. Molinard's voice is a singular one. Her writing is disturbing and heartbreaking, fascinating and compulsively readable, teetering on the edge of, and then plunging fully into, insanity. Her stories are moody, manic, sad, erratic—hovering somewhere between the longing to make others understand how Molinard saw the world and the simple need to express a particular worldview, an acute instability of mind. They are full of odd twists and turns that often go nowhere or bring you right back to where you started, like tiny nightmares. Full of characters who don't seem to be aware of just how warped their realities are and instead doggedly persist in playing the game. And full of strange and frantic realities, stifling existences where nothing seems to follow any kind of logic. They are absurdist, bizarre, and unlike anything else I've read.

Each story recounts a haunting, sometimes upsetting or surreal experience, usually focused on one character whose world appears normal until suddenly something shifts and we realize everything has slipped out of control, or maybe their tenuous grasp on reality was never there to begin with. "The Plane from Santa Rosa" begins with a woman at the airport asking about the time the plane from Santa Rosa will arrive, how many stops it will make, the length of each one. She has much to prepare. She rushes around the rest of the afternoon, trying on dress after dress, fur after fur; there's no time for tailoring, everything has to be just right for her friends, the dinner, that very night. She hurries back to the airport and watches every passenger get off the plane until she is alone in the deserted terminal. In "The Meeting," a man takes a train to an unknown town and immediately gets lost. He grows increasingly disoriented and decides to walk with his hand on a high wall that never seems to end to ensure he doesn't get turned around. This goes on for months. Eventually he tries scaling the wall. In "The Vault," Molinard narrates to Duras how the sight of a vault in a cemetery inspires her with the obsessive idea to sleep inside it for three days. She makes all the necessary preparations and is on her way until her husband and doctor intervene. Then she starts to feel pains all over her body, realizing these are the pains she would have felt had she slept on the floor of the vault for those three nights.

"The Headless Man" tells the story of a woman who finds herself sitting on the same bench every day, watching people pass and transform abruptly before her eyes into monstrous, grotesque animals. Then she encounters THE HEADLESS MAN, who promises to help her in her ever-thwarted quest to make the 5:30 p.m. train, which she can never seem to reach in time. In "The Cage," the longest story in the collection, a woman named Berthe, who is unspeakably lonely, walks through a zoo, distraught by the sight of the animals in their cages. She finds happiness at last when she meets a man and they fall madly in love. But one day he insists on taking her to the zoo, where he develops an obsession with a snake after he hallucinates that the snake is trying to communicate something important to him.

From story to story, each character's voice is unique,

but they all share a form of madness, an overarching blur of the real and the absurd, believable enough to be frightening. In my translation, I paid particular attention to heeding each character's specific sense of the world while honoring the book's distinctive unsettling tone and Molinard's startling use of small caps and atypical punctuation to heighten this uncanny atmosphere. These stories may have been intended to impose order on the chaos of Molinard's mind, but they also alert her readers to the inner workings of a tortured spirit that can't seem to find peace; a world of little panics.

It's easy to compare Molinard to writers like Katherine Mansfield, Franz Kafka, or Leonora Carrington, but she's also nothing like them, because as Duras says in her preface, these stories are not invented or dreamed—they are LIVED. Molinard did not conjure up insanity; it existed within her. *Panics* is a challenging, mesmerizing book. It is not writing that aims to please, or that aims for prizes or praise. Barbara Molinard wrote what she needed to write for herself, to get by, to make it through each day, to tolerate the experience of being alive. She wrote through her mental anguish in a way that is palpable on the page, in a way that not many writers, let alone women writers, have dared to do. *Panics* is a book that could only have been written by Barbara Molinard, for Barbara Molinard. Her voice is a valuable, searing addition to the literary landscape, and especially to the landscape of literature in translation. I believe firmly that awards and recognitions do not determine an author's worthiness of being translated. That the connection and passion a translator has for an author and their book are testament enough to a book's merit, to its ability to touch readers and spur them to question their own realities. That an author's ferocious, urgent need to write can be enough to propel them to other worlds, other languages, and new readers. I can't think of a better home for this book than Feminist Press, which has long been doing the work of recovering lost literature by women writers.

As soon as I read *Viens*, I reached out to Barbara Molinard's daughter Agnès, who generously agreed to meet with me in Paris when I visited a few months later. In the years since then, Agnès has sent me postcards, early morning WhatsApp updates, and countless emails. She has seen the evolution of this translation coincide with momentous changes in my life. She welcomed me into her home during a lull period in the pandemic, talked to me about her mother, asked me about my parents, who live not far from her in France, and shared her mother's drawings and paintings, which are just as haunting as her writing. I am extremely grateful to Agnès for all of her aid, trust, and patience as this book came together in English.

As I write this note, I am recovering from an illness that left me feeling like my head had come unscrewed for days on end. I experienced it as a frightening shift in myself, my thoughts, my reality. I was haunted by the idea that I might not recover, that this warped world would be my new permanent state. As I slowly return to the familiarity of my mind, I am left wondering: Is this how Barbara Molinard felt?

The truth is that I'll never know how Molinard felt,

or what exactly lived in her mind. What's clear is that Molinard was a tortured woman with no regard for fame or recognition, and that her book might well have stayed forgotten. But by a miraculous set of circumstances, something else happened instead. Now Barbara Molinard's *Panics* will live on the shelves of English-language readers, and may soon also appear in further editions abroad. Perhaps most exciting, *Viens* will have a new publication in French this year, by Éditions Cambourakis, to accompany the English-language edition. Sometimes as translators, we are tasked with translating the shiny new thing, the prizewinning book, a publisher's latest lead title. Sometimes, instead, we are destined to cross paths with a long-forgotten book and steal it away from that other, most formidable enemy—oblivion.

—Emma Ramadan
Providence, RI
March 2022

Barbara Molinard (1921–1986) wrote and wrote, but published only one book in her lifetime. Everything she wrote, she immediately tore to shreds; it was only through the relentless urging from her husband, the filmmaker Patrice Molinard, and her friend Marguerite Duras, that she finally handed over a single collection of stories, *Viens*, to Éditions Mercure de France in 1969.

Emma Ramadan translates books of all genres from French. Her translations include Anne Garréta's *Sphinx*, Virginie Despentes's *Pretty Things*, and Abdellah Taïa's *A Country for Dying*.

More Translated Literature from the Feminist Press

La Bastarda by Trifonia Melibea Obono, translated by Lawrence Schimel

Beijing Comrades by Bei Tong, translated by Scott E. Myers

Black Box: The Memoir That Sparked Japan's #MeToo Movement by Shiori Ito, translated by Allison Markin Powell

Blood Feast: The Complete Short Stories of Malika Moustadraf translated by Alice Guthrie

Cockfight by María Fernanda Ampuero, translated by Frances Riddle

Grieving: Dispatches from a Wounded Country by Cristina Rivera Garza, translated by Sarah Booker

In Case of Emergency by Mahsa Mohebali, translated by Mariam Rahmani

The Living Days by Ananda Devi, translated by Jeffrey Zuckerman

Mars: Stories by Asja Bakić, translated by Jennifer Zoble

Pretty Things by Virginie Despentes, translated by Emma Ramadan

Testo Junkie: Sex, Drugs, and Biopolitics in the Pharmacopornographic Era by Paul B. Preciado, translated by Bruce Benderson

Violets by Kyung-Sook Shin, translated by Anton Hur

The Feminist Press publishes books that ignite movements and social transformation. Celebrating our legacy, we lift up insurgent and marginalized voices from around the world to build a more just future.

See our complete list of books at
feministpress.org

THE FEMINIST PRESS
AT THE CITY UNIVERSITY OF NEW YORK
FEMINISTPRESS.ORG